The soldier made me think of a donkey with a pannier; his back support ___ ___ on either end, and in each ___ ___ ___ one dark.

He stopped when he re___ ___ ___ King's shepherd. "The___ ___ ___ ___ tor," he said, handing the bar to the grizzled old man. "Babies grow up to become princes. Princes lead rebellions and fulfill prophecies. The King wants you to drown them."

The shepherd nodded. "Yes. The King is wise. I tend sheep, but I am also a priest of the goddess Rumina. To kill princes, Amulius would choose a priest—and one in the country, so the deed will not be known in town. Yes, I will give them to the Tiber."

Luperca and I exchanged glances. We knew what must be done. Still . . . a Dryad and a she-wolf—we were hardly a promising team for the rescue of the twins.

THOMAS BURNETT SWANN

LADY
OF THE BEES

ace books
A Division of Charter Communications Inc.
1120 Avenue of the Americas
New York, N.Y. 10036

LADY OF THE BEES

An ACE Book

First ACE printing: May, 1976

Printed in U.S.A.

DEDICATION

TO STELLA STEVENS, STAR

Inimitable in beauty, incomparable in genius,
love goddess to a godless age

HISTORICAL NOTE

The degree of civilization reflected in this novel, the architecture of temples and palaces, the sculpture of images exquisite in gold or malachite, the religion of humanized deities with great personal beauty and a very personal interest in nubile princesses, even the calendar divided into twelve months, did not belong to the relatively primitive peoples who created Rome. Rather, I have followed the Roman poets in idealizing their past. Most modern historians contend that Romulus and Remus were merely myths; that the first settlers on the Palatine were illiterate shepherds and thieves; that Rome, far from being founded, grew haphazardly from a village of wattle huts into a city of concrete, bricks, and marble. They are doubtless right.

Still, poetry and fiction possess a truth which eludes history: to interpret rather than record. My novel is an interpretation.

MELLONIA

I

My name is Mellonia, the Dryad, though the Fauns have named me the "Perpetual Virgin" in a forest where virginity is as rare and reprehensible as promiscuity among the humans of Alba Longa. The Lemur or ghost of my Aunt Segeta adds the damning words, "By choice."

True, I have had two lovers.

"But that was in the time of Saturn, wasn't it?" Segeta insists.

"No," I protest. "It was much, much later. It was four hundred and fifty-three years ago—*you* should remember—when I lost my maidenhead to Aeneas in a hollow tree."

"All the same, Niece," she shrugs, "you've had sufficient time to grow a new one. And what, by Sylvanus' holy rod, are you saving it for? Don't make my mistake. I was a mere fifteen males short of being a virgin when I died. You may recall that I started rather late."

"I'm saving it for Mercury when he comes to guide me to the Underworld. Or Charon. After all, I have to buy my passage across the Styx."

"It won't buy you a ride with the Gray Ferryman. He's older, they say, than Saturn. You'll wander the

Nether Lands like me. Besides, nobody knows for sure that there *is* another side to the Styx."

"The Elysian Fields—"

"An invention of poets. Much too pretty to be believed. To me, the Styx resembles an ocean with only one shore. Ask any Lemur. He will tell you the same."

"Very well then, I'm saving it for another Aeneas, another Ascanius."

"The waste, the wicked waste," she mutters, gazing upon me with horror and fascination. "Four hundred and seventy years of Dryad in the body of a young woman. Streaks of age in your hair, but gold, by Aphrodite's girdle, instead of a mossy silver! You may not be the slip of a girl Aeneas loved, and after him that splendid young warrior, his son Ascanius, but you're a woman all right—four feet of walking temptation, full breasts, curving hips, and you still look *young,* though your tree must have sheltered Saturn. You might at least get fat or gather a few wrinkles or grow knock-kneed. As it is, you walk about like a fig tree ripe for plucking, but no, your fruits are not for the likes of a Faun—scroungy, you call him—or a human, unless he happens to be a great hero, and great heroes, my dear, do not belong to the present age. I don't even meet them in the Nether Lands."

"Perhaps they have found a way to cross the Styx," I say, adding, "I will cook you a meal." I feel by now as if I ought to wear sackcloth or crop my hair to atone for my chastity ."Lentils and beans?"

She looks prepared to disdain such plebeian fare;

she deigns. "Oh, very well. I do feel a trifle immaterial." She can neither chew nor digest, but she encompasses and absorbs the food with the amethyst mist, translucent and billowing, which has replaced her body, and she gains sufficient sustenance to resume her admonishment. A single bean lingers and revolves in what should have been her stomach.

"If you don't choose a lover, and soon, Venus will nip you in the bud. Listen to old Segeta. You'll see!"

"Ah," I mutter, "if only she would," but amethyst mist, it seems, is hard of hearing (like certain goddesses).

With Fauns in the woods and men in the nearest town, Alba Longa, I usually keep to my tree, notwithstanding admonitions from a ghost. I do have my visitors. The Telesphori come to ask me the herbs and simples I use to keep what they call, in their formal and stately diction, my pulchritude. Shy little healers in muffling green hoods, they show their faces and feet, pink as the throat of a conch shell, but you have to guess their tails. A bear escaping from hunters may find a refuge at my table, in spite of his uncouth manners. Bees spin circles around my windows to tell me of honeycombs in hollow logs. Even woodpeckers, usually the scourge of oaks, rest on my limbs without hammering a nest. But Fauns are as disagreeable as a thunderstorm. And men—well, men have diminished since Ascanius' day. Not in number; not, alas, in size. Indeed, they have multiplied and, wearing helmets, they look like Achilles and Ajax and other giants from that giant and tragic war, the siege of Troy. What they have lost is the valor, what they have lost is the vision, which they brought with their household gods from their fallen city. Belated Trojans, they have forgotten Troy. I am not afraid of them. I am not concerned with them.

In a moment of rare self-pity—increasingly frequent, I fear—I confide in the young she-wolf, lately a cub, whom I saved from a table set by hungry Fauns.

"Luperca, Venus has surely cursed me, just as Segeta threatened, though in quite the opposite way. Instead of nipping my bud, she has afflicted me with eternal bloom. I found you only a cub; now you are a yearling; fifteen years from now you will be a grizzled old wolf, and then you will go to your rest. I alone have broken the ancient cycle of winter burgeoning into spring and summer subsiding into the sweet oblivion of autumn. Who is so much enamored with morning that she can endure the glare of the sun while civilizations reach their titan hands to grasp the sky and falter empty-handed into the dust?"

Luperca sniffs impatiently for her dinner. She does not approve of my high-flown lamentations.

"Oh, very well," I say, petulant at the loss of my audience. "I shall fix you a stew of squirrels and sparrowgrass. I know you dislike the second, but the first will make you fat, and mates are scarce these days—

at least for wolves." Luperca opens her mouth and lolls her tongue.

"Patience, good daughter. Yes, you prefer your squirrels uncooked, but you are my guest. You must eat what I choose to prepare."

I hear a persistent knocking on my tree.

Pestiferous woodpeckers, how many times have I told them to light but not to knock——

It is not a woodpecker, it is a Faun. I can tell as he kicks my trunk with his cloven hoof.

Angrily I open a circular window block, confront a stranger, and laugh in his face. . . .

II

Like all of his race, whatever their age, he resembles a comical child. He gapes at me as if I were about to switch him with a hazel rod; at the same time, I read the eternal mischief of the Faun: a child's mind, a boy's cunning, an old man's lust.

"I don't know your name," I say. "I know what you want."

"May I have it? My name is Nemustrinus. Come down from your trees." My window is high above his head.

"What will you give me?"

"Pleasure, what else?" He seems to forget that his odor of stale fish, and his coarse hair, matted with dirt and brambles, are not enticing to every woman.

I have learned to make a weapon of banter. "I must be bought."

"You sound like a human girl," he complains. "The Lemur of my great-great-great-uncle—I forget the number of greats"—Fauns can never add—"tells me that in the reign of Saturn, every Dryad thought it enough to be pleasured by a Faun. If he brought her a gift, why, she took him into her tree. Two gifts and he could stay for a month."

"I did not live in the time of Saturn. In my own time, however, I was a queen and my subjects numbered a hundred or more, and our circle of oaks, the Wanderwood, was stronger than any fort. We *never* coupled with Fauns. True, the days of my reign are gone, and so are my subjects, victims of plague and blight and the axes of heartless men. I am quite alone among the tenantless trees. Still, I refuse to couple with a Faun."

"Oh," he said. "You must be Mellonia. I know about *you*."

"What do you know?"

"The *virgin*." He might have said whore.

"I have had two lovers. I hardly qualify."

"That was an eternity ago." Fauns age more quickly than humans, much more quickly than Dryads, and count themselves blessed to achieve their twentieth year.

"I have a long memory."

"I could do you a favor. I could take you to the burying."

"What sort of burying?"

"That's my secret. It's among the humans of Alba Longa, though." He is young for a Faun, eighteen months old at the most; his face, if you ignore the horns, is not uncomely, though the lips are thick, the nostrils flat and flaring; his chest is a copse instead of a forest, but the flanks, those hirsute horrors which all of his race inherit from their patron deity, Faunus —well, I could never endure them. Does it come from their diet of refuse and sour milk?

"Such a long walk," I temporized.

"Why, you can outrun a deer. That's how you've kept your maidenhead. The one that grew back."

"I won't promise," I said, curious in spite of myself. I envisioned a princely treasure about to be buried by thieves, a sunburst of gold and electrum, a tiara of malachite. I envisioned the burial of a great personage among the humans, a king or a queen, and hornets of envy assaulted me, a longing to watch (or even replace?).

Perhaps I would stroke his ears in return for his gift. Perhaps I would ask him to a supper of sorel and fennel stalks, though not in my tree. I could almost forget that a Faun had killed Aeneas.

"I won't promise, but come, show me your burying."

7

"Quiet now," he said. "No one must see us. Fauns are no more welcome than goats in Alba Longa; they mistake us for thieves."

"And rightly so."

He looked at me with his slanted goat eyes. "You know what they do to Dryads."

"Put them into a circus." The Alba Longans had copied their circuses from the Etruscans. There were conjurings of the dead, divinations from the entrails of a sheep, duels between men and animals, wrestling matches. There were shows in which sea-born Tritons were floated in tanks of river water (until they died) and Centaurs were chained to chariots and forced to race (they generally broke their necks). They had captured my Aunt Segeta for just such a wanton display. Away from her tree, she had died within a week, as brittle and brown as an autumn-crisped leaf.

Alba Longa was not a second Troy, if I could judge from Aeneas' description. Still, it was great and terrifying to me—a fortified mound with crenellated, turreted walls of cyclopean rocks, and massive bronze gates which resembled a Cyclops' jaws. The roofs of platformed temples, Etruscan style, peaked sharply above the walls. A road of basalt blocks, the Sacred Way, serpentined from the gates between rows of cypresses, skirted the woods and led through open fields and herds and grassy hills to Veii, the City of a Thousand Images. Warriors afoot or in chariots constantly patrolled the roads and the forest did not encroach, it shrank like a wounded squid and gathered concealing thicknesses to hide its folk. I found the thicket closest to the road and trusted the green of my hair to pass for leaves, the gold for asters or daffodils. Nemustrinus, crouched and hairy, resembled a strayed goat.

A long procession descended the avenue, proceeded and flanked by guards, those men with bronze greaves and tall, iron-tipped spears, and eyes as cold as the metals in their armor. Where was the casket or catafalque? No, I recalled, the men of Alba Longa cremated their dead. Where was the funerary urn? I could only see the Vestal Virgins, those white immaculate flames, and a man enrobed in purple—the king's color—with a sharp black beard like a wedge and slanted Etruscan eyes. I recognized Amulius. He had stolen the throne from his brother, Numitor, the benign if absentminded astrologer who had studied the stars before every decision of state and, indeed, was studying Gemini when Amulius' soldiers seized the throne. Amulius kept him a prisoner in the palace except, as now, when he wished to parade him before the people who, having prospered under his docile rule, would have resented his death. His neatly trimmed beard—trimmed, no doubt, by the King's barber —and ruddy countenance—ruddied no doubt with carmine by the King's eunuch—gave him the look of a guest instead of a prisoner.

And the girl. . . .

Ah, she might have been me when I lost Aeneas— young beyond belief, stricken, but proud in her innocence (I knew her innocent). They had shackled her wrists; they could not shackle her pride. I always judge a person by his eyes. Bad men veil their thoughts, and yet I can stare out malice, theft, rape. I look behind the eyes. Aeneas' eyes were azure bits of sky; they seemed to yearn for their celestial home. Some dismissed him as an ineffectual dreamer; I saw the bronze behind the dreams. Ascanius' eyes were gray. Hard, said his enemies. "A rough piratical fellow," he liked to laugh. I saw the loving son, the devoted brother, the faithful lover. This girl's eyes, black in the noonday sun, revealed her as inexperienced in the ways of men, but one who would never willingly have renounced the world and become a cloistered Vestal. Amulius had given her to the Goddess when he dethroned her father. Now, it seemed, he thought her a threat.

"Nemustrinus," I whispered. "She is Numitor's daughter, Rhea Silva, descended from my own Ascanius!" In spite of his love for me, Aeneas' son had taken a mortal wife to give him a human heir. The son I had borne Aeneas had died of a chill because of his Dryad blood. Ascanius would not let me bear him a child who was "half of the forest, half of the town, belonging wholly to neither."

"Yes," said Nemustrinus, expectant of his reward. "But what has she done?"

"Watch!"

I saw a soldier who made me think of a donkey

with a pannier; his back supporter a bar, the bar a basket on either end, and in each basket, an infant boy, one fair, one dark.

"But Rhea was a Novice, a holy girl." Even in my tree, a half day's walk from the town, I learned such things from the Forest Folk. "She would have become a Vestal."

"Yes," he grinned. "To honor Vesta, the Hearthfire. Vesta, the Virgin."

"And yet this Novice, this would-be Vestal——"

"Bore twins a month ago."

"Who is the father?"

"Mars, the girl insists. He came to her in a dream. A young artisan, says Amulius. There was a trial. There was a witness. The boy was beheaded. See? On the stake before the gate."

The head was unrecognizable. The vultures, birds of good omen among the Alba Longans, had been encouraged to feast.

"I believe her," I said. "Gods *do* descend. . . ." I thought of Aeneas, the son of Venus.

"And men climb in windows," he laughed. At first I had tolerated him; now I despised him. My fingers tightened around the onyx dagger I wore in my sash.

"And they are going to——"

"Bury her."

Stupid, stupid! Where was my vaunted intuition? I had willingly followed him to a burial, not of a treasure, not of a dead queen, but of a living girl.

11

"See!" he exulted, his pointed ears aquiver like those of a goat with flies. "That mound of earth——"

"Hush. Do you think I'm blind?"

They had dug her tomb beside the Sacred Way, at the foot of a hill. They would give her a stone and inscription befitting a princess, no doubt. Even a fallen Vestal, even the daughter of a deposed king, required propriety from her murderers.

The tomb was a chamber cut into dirt and rock and containing, I guessed, a couch and a small supply of food and water. According to law, Amulius was not allowed to execute a Novice convicted of fornication; he could, however, must, however, allow her to die. His men would cover the roof with a wooden plank and shovel the plank with earth. First, they would insert a wooden tube to supply her with air. She would not suffocate; she would die of thirst or fear.

No, not fear, this girl with the eyes of a queen, this girl who had taken no vintner into her couch. A god, or one who passed for a god, had been her beloved.

They removed the thongs to release her hands. She held them up to the light, pale, small, perfect. Turning, she faced her accusers, her sometime friends, her helpless, hapless father. She did not plead; she simply stated her innocence.

"He came to me in a shower of gold, like Zeus to Danaë. But I knew him for Mars at once. Patron of farmers, lord of battles. He hadn't a beard, you see, and his hair was as gold as a shield in the sun. My hair is as black as the earth with which you will seal my tomb. That poor young man you beheaded—I never knew his name. I saw him from time to time in the streets and he bowed to my sisters and me with reverence in his eyes, not lust. His hair was black like mine. Look at my sons."

"The boy confessed," said Amulius. His voice resembled the hoot of an owl, a sound which passes for wisdom when no one bothers to understand that the bird is saying, "Me, me, me."

"Under torture."

"Of his own will, before witnesses. Do you think that a god—especially the Holy Father Mars—would violate a Vestal?"

"He did not violate me. He spoke my name. 'Rhea,' he said. 'Give me sons to build my city.' I opened my arms to him."

Numitor, silent till now, dazed, I think, spoke like a man returned from the Styx. "Aeneas predicted just such a city."

"Alba Longa."

"No, a greater. A second Troy." He stirred from his dream. A sleepwalker awakened (or one who even in grief retained his sense of royalty, the noble gesture, the way of kings?), he threaded between the guards and took his daughter into his arms. No one tried to stop him.

"Father, it will be well with me. The God has promised!" She clung to him, briefly a little girl, but returned to womanhood and a woman's death. She kissed his cheek and walked, without compulsion, to the edge of the pit. Lifting her arms, she stared at the sky.

"So blue, so blue," she said, half in a whisper, and yet we heard her as if she had shouted the words. "It overarches the world like the wing of a god. I must memorize its blue."

Foot under tiny foot, she descended the ladder into the tomb. Amulius nodded and slaves, unobtrusive in brown loincloths, emerged from the crowd and proceeded to bury the door. The dirt which rained from their shovels reenacted, in miniature, the lava from Mt. Vesuvius, that son of Vulcan, in one of his shows of rage.

Numitor gave a single anguished cry, "Rhea!", and swooned, so it seemed to me, with a guard conveniently at hand to break his fall.

"Earth, reclaim your errant daughter," intoned Amulius. "Vesta, cleanse her of guilt with your all-pervasive fire." He has the eyes of an owl, I thought, and owls are never wise, whatever men think, but cunning to capture the mouse or the squirrel.

"Now I shall claim my reward," said the Faun, grasping my shoulder. "Did you ever see such a sight? The burial of a princess!"

He was no longer a comical child. He had torn the wings from a butterfly. I shook free of him. He groped for my arm—I felt his hairy fingers through

14

the sleeve of my tunic—and I struck him across the mouth. He did not follow me.

I followed the donkey-faced guard with the twins.

III

"Drown them, Faustulus," he said, handing them to the shepherd who, I recalled, had tended the herds of Numitor, now the herds of Amulius. I had followed the guard and a well-worn cattle trail from the city of temples to a village of wattle huts. A wall of wooden stakes, anathema to wolves, enclosed the huts, together with pens for fastidious pigs and rancid goats, and a small enclosure of cypress wood, roofless but sacrosanct, dedicated to Rumina, the goddess of nursing mothers.

I had climbed a rowan tree and I peered from its branches like a wren from a nest. Safe, so I thought. Seeing but unseen.

"The King has told his people that he has sent the boys to live with a kinsman in Etruria. But of course they must die. Babies grow up. Princes may lead rebellions to avenge mothers or fulfill prophecies."

Faustulus nodded and rather too eagerly, I thought, accepted the children into his arms.

"Yes," he said, between a growl and a grunt. "I

will give them to the Tiber. He will swallow them like a serpent."

"And I will watch him feast. I must carry word to the King that I have seen them drown."

You would like to see them drown. You are worse than a cruel and childish Faun. You are a cruel young man.

"Be off with you, Celer. Do you think I would disobey him? He would have my head on a stake!" Faustulus was tall and formidable; aging but hardly old; a leader by virtue of strength as well as years. His skin was the color and texture of bark; his beard was moss, graying but not yet gray. He was called the Oak.

He clenched a massive fist to enforce his words. Shepherds paused in the doors to their huts—poised, I should say—to await his command. Firelight illumined them into figures of bronze, no, of wood. The forest was in their craggy faces, their knotted arms; like trees, they stood tall; like trees, they offered protection instead of invasion.

Celer glared at him and turned reluctantly in his tracks, muttering, "I will say that I watched them drown."

He saw me in my tree as he left the camp. I read his eyes: behind his donkey face, the long head, the large ears, lay the soul of a serval cat, that sleek and treacherous animal beloved as a pet by Etruscan kings. He did not recognize me for a Dryad. The marks of my race, the tunic, the green hair, the pointed ears, were hidden by leaves and branches. Perhaps he mistook me for a shepherd's girl. Lust disfigured his face into the mask of a mime. He grinned; his grin was at once an invitation and a threat: Accept or submit.

At first I thought that he meant to climb the tree. But the camp was much too close. The shepherds could hear my cries (or so he must have thought. He could not see my knife).

"Later," I heard him say, half in promise, half in anger. The chatter of magpies muffled his steps. He was not worth our fear. I returned to my watch.

I was ready to call from the tree and forbid the execution. These shepherds, I knew, had always respected the Forest Folk. I would identify myself as Aeneas' love and claim the twins.

But I saw in Faustulus' eyes that he did not mean to obey Amulius.

"Here, here, little ones," he said with the rough and hesitant friendliness of a man unused to children. "Hungry, are you? My wife, Larentia, shall give you some milk."

She emerged from the hut—materialized—a wraith of a woman whose footsteps were whispers; whose robe of plain homespun seemed somehow woven of night. She was not, however, her husband's shadow.

"Faustulus, you are not to kill them."

"I have been expecting Celer," he said. "I knew the charge he would bring me. Amulius is a tyrant but also, strangely, a man in awe of the gods. I am a shepherd but also a priest to Rumina. To murder

17

princes, he would only choose a priest. The deed must not be known in the town; therefore, he chose from his shepherds in the country."

"By Saturn's mossy beard, I wonder the gods can abide your prayers! You deliver speeches instead of sentences. What about the twins?"

"I have made them a boat out of osier reeds."

"Why can't we keep them here? Amulius never visits the village. Rarely sends his men. Two little boys are easily hidden."

"I have sworn to give them to the river. I cannot break my oath as a priest, even to the hireling of a tyrant. But if the river should return their boat. . . ."

She laughed like the wind as it plays with a nest of wrens, a young mother's laugh. "A man and his pride! I would have sworn and broken a hundred oaths to save those boys. Well, we shall pray to the Forest Folk. If any are left. We have frightened them with our axes and our roads. Amulius' men have hunted them for his circuses."

"Shepherds have never harmed them, my dear. We have left libations of honey at hollow trees. Given Rumina the milk from the whitest cows. Come, we will stand and raise our arms in prayer."

"For sons?" she asked. "It is not too much to ask? Princes at that."

"Rumina, goddess of nursing mothers. . . ."

"Follow them, Luperca, you on that side, I on this.

We shall wait till they drift ashore." Needless to say, I had never learned to swim. Wooden vibrations are lost to rapid waters, and Dryads avoid a river as Naiads a forest. Luperca had swum to the opposite bank, but only under the threat of a hazel switch and the bribe of a raw squirrel. Between us, we were hardly a promising team for the rescue of the twins.

Fortunately, the Tiber is not a ferocious river except in flood; in places he is little more than a stream. He dealt gently with the twins; he nudged, twisted, lifted their osier cockleshell of a boat, but he did not try to swamp; at length, he wafted them among the reeds ahead of me. Dragonflies—crimson bodies and silver wings—spurted out of my path and hung, an aerial garden, as I parted the reeds. Luperca sought the narrowest ford and joined me, shaking free of the water as if it were pitch from one of the burning lakes to the north. Black Hair squalled like a wolf cub, angry, not afraid.

"You are Luperca's," I said. "I will call you the Little Wolf."

Fair Hair happily made a nest of my arms. He smelled of osiers and lily pads.

"And you—I will name you after a bird. Aeneas was Halcyon, Ascanius was Phoenix. My son was Cuckoo. You are Woodpecker, I think. The Bird of Fire. Your hair is yellow instead of red. Still, both of you are flames."

I tried to love them the same, the fair and the dark,

for in both I recognized the unmistakable touch of divinity. But the heart, like a bird, accepts no commands. I loved the fair; I feared the dark.

Luperca at my heels, I cradled both of them in my arms and started the journey to my tree. Behind us, sandals crackled along the river bank—shepherds, no doubt, in search of what I had already found. I laughed at my successful theft.

Sometimes I had to rest. The twins were large for their age. I was small as humans measure size. Once I gave them water from trumpet flowers. Fair Hair drank the water and kept his flower; Dark Hair drank and threw his flower to the ground. At last, and yet too soon—for I enjoyed my bundles—we reached my tree. Woodpeckers, bears, wolf cubs. . . . Why should I not rear the human kin of my own Ascanius?

"Home," I said. Dark Hair looked at my tree with curiosity and grudging approval. Fair Hair clung to my neck and took the word on faith.

"First, I must give my thanks to Rumina. Of all the goddesses, she only has time for babes in arms."

"Niece!" Segeta, who else?

For once I could not show respect, even for blood, even for the dead. "Hush, Old Woman. You will frighten my twins. Why can't you leave me alone? I know you're restless in the Nether Lands, but must you always come at the wrong time with the wrong advice?"

"Ungrateful child," she clucked. "Honor my years if not my experience. If you rear them as Dryad children they will come to love your tree, which is all very well. They will come to depend on your tree, which isn't. How can they ever return to Alba Longa? And return they must, for they are princes and there is a throne to claim. Consider Cuckoo, your son."

"Cuckoo lived to be twenty-five. He died of a chill."

"He died from the demons of town and marketplace. His Dryad blood——"

"He was happy until he died. There are worse things than death at twenty-five."

"He took no bride. Bore no children. *He* knew the risk. *He* knew the power of a tree—to protect, but only so long as you stay within its citadel."

"These are sturdy boys. They are one month old. They could pass for six. I hardly expect my tree to weaken their blood. Return to your wanderings and leave me to my sons."

Needless to say, the door to my tree was not in the trunk; it is cruel to cut holes into living wood (even my windows are cut into sapless parts). Furthermore, obvious doors invite visitors—and invaders.

Gently I laid the boys at Luperca's feet. She crouched above them as if she would like to give suck, though of course she was still too young. Acanthus lilies and jonquils hid the place; Rumina's altar too, scattered by many weathers (but not its sacredness). I parted the flowers and knelt; I lifted a door so cleverly colored and contoured that even animals mistook it for a rock.

Carrying two babies, of course, I could not descend a ladder, walk through the tunnel under the tree, and ascend the spiral stairs within the trunk.

"Luperca—"

I did not have to give her instructions. As daintily as if she were carrying a squab to a hungry cub, she lifted Black Hair by the seat of his loin cloth and felt her way down the slanted ladder.

"Never mind," I whispered to his twin. "You shall travel with me."

How warm and familiar he felt against my breast, how sturdily beat his heart!

"You are not like my Cuckoo at all. He was always a sickly child, though I loved him the more for every demon he fought, and loved him the most at the last."

We followed Luperca into the tree. With one hand I held the child; with the other I lowered the door which shut us into the cool and familiar night of roots and earth.

How can a tree survive with a tunnel bored in its trunk, and rooms atop the tunnel? But 'bored' is the wrong word. 'Grown,' I should say. Some oaks grow with large and elaborate hollows, designed, it would seem, to be occupied into houses. Lacking a Dryad, the tree will die in a single night. If we are nourished by emanations of leaf and bark and wood, so too is the tree sustained by our warmth, our motion, our love. We are separate entities and yet we are one: Father Tree and Daughter Dryad. (It is part of Venus' pattern, the variegated mosaic of life which only I have broken with my unseasonable youth.)

And so we came into my atrium, my house-place. Once I remove the window blocks, the sun tiptoes into the room and touches the Adonis-pots, the diminutive pool of water carried laboriously from tulip flowers and swimming with tadpoles which, matured into frogs, will sweeten the air with song. Above me is the room where I cook on the brazier and eat my berries and mushrooms; twice above me, the room which keeps my couch, my cedar chest, my tunics, the bow which belonged to Aeneas, Ascanius' favorite knife. . . .

But here in the atrium, I fed the twins. Where did I find the food? There are no secrets among the Forest Folk. It was they who brought the food.

"Listen," I said to the twins. "A woodpecker is pounding on my walls! Often they are petulant and disagreeable birds, who hammer holes in our trees. But this one is a particular friend. I know him by his knock. His crest is red, his breast is green, and he would have me believe that he is the god Picus, changed to a bird by Circe, the enchantress, when he scorned her love. But woodpeckers rival Fauns with their tall tales. Still, I call him Picus to save his pride."

Picus had brought a gift of berries in his claws. Red, sweet, succulent, they were known as forest-fond and fed to cubs and babies and even the young of the Telesphori, who hang from trees like pears. Black Hair examined suspiciously, snatched, and devoured; Fair Hair opened his mouth and waited until he was fed. Picus preened his feathers in satisfaction.

Meanwhile, Luperca had left the tree—she can open the hidden door from the inside with her head, from the outside with her teeth—and now she returned with something more sustaining than berries: a wooden pail (Cuckoo had made it, his first gift to me) with milk from one of her friends, a she-wolf with cubs.

Luperca was the first; she was not the last. A gentle procession brought more gifts to the twins: bees with royal jelly; a bear with a raw fish which I secretly fed to Luperca, since bears know nothing of human diet (they mean well, though); finally, three of the Telesphori, each with a special gift more lasting than food. One brought nectar distilled from columbine and sweater than myrrh; one brought a minuscule golden box with an image carved from malachite, the gem most valued among the folk in the green forest; one, more practical if less artistic than his friends, brought a pair of tunics precisely fitted to the size of the twins.

The Telesphori live in the Valley of the Blue Monkeys. Their hooded figures reflect the secrecy of their land. It is ruled by a king who sits on a throne of teakwood and takes tea while he dispenses justice. It is a land of wind chimes sweeter than lyres and strange animals like piebald bears, and trees which grow like intertwining snakes. It is a valley but also a way. The Telesphori exchange gifts as other folk exchange truths.

I opened a chest and removed the cradle which I had kept since Cuckoo was a baby, a large inverted tortoise shell on wooden rockers, and the bringers of gifts came in turn to visit the twins in their swaddling clothes, then in their tunics, and wish them health and prosperity.

"And a throne," said the chief of the Telesphori, the bringer of tunics. A child pretending a throne for other children, I thought, when I looked at his pink, boyish countenance enwreathed by his green hood. Then I remembered to look behind his eyes and saw a thousand years of sadnesses beyond number, though always confronted with courage, and I knew that he had chosen his wish as carefully as a king chooses his crown.

A rat seemed to gnaw at my heart.

"Please," I said. "They are sleepy now. Who will sing them a lullaby?"

"I will," said the smallest, shyest Telesphorus, he who had brought the golden box and the image of malachite. "You see, it is a god who lies in the box. Vaticanus, the friend of children. Whether they hang from a tree like my brothers, or lie in a cradle of tortoise-shell. Here. I will wake him." He held the figure against the light: boy-god; tunic, sandals, filleted hair; a spray of wheat like a wand in his outstretched hand. He sang this song in my ear:

> Little laughing flaxen lad,
> Lad of ebony,

Nothing touch thee, bad nor sad,
Safe within thy father tree.

"And what is your gift, Good Sister?" asked the singer.

"I have saved it for last," I said.

I took them by night, clothed in their new tunics, fragrant with columbine, and rich with golden box and image of malachite, and rapped at the door of Faustulus' hut.

"Luperca," I said. "Look after my sons. Stay with Larentia and help her to raise them as princes—both of them, not just Romulus. She will read your name on the sheet of papyrus I have hung from your neck." I had written:

A god sired them;
A she-wolf fed them;
A woodpecker brought them berries.
Can you do less?

Then I returned to my tree and dreamed of snow.

SYLVAN

I

My people, the Fauns, belong to the countryside and not the town. Since Faunus, our divine ancestor, sired our race on a shapely mountain goat, we have wandered the blue-rocked Apennines where the Tiber coils from his secret lair in the earth and swells with the melting snow on his way to the sea; we have roamed the forests of beech and oak and red-berried rowan where Dryads comb green hair and the Telesphori, wise children with ancient hearts, muffle themselves in hoods like snails in shells, and remember Saturn, King of the Golden Age.

A wanderer's life should not encumber him. Shaggy as goats, what do we need with robes except, in the winter sleep, a wolf-skin to warm our shoulders against the cold? We have no weapons except a simple sling with a hempen cord, a bane to wolves. We have no women unless we entice the maidens out of their high-walled towns, the Dryads out of their trees. My own mother—I forget her name—was a maiden of Alba Longa who met my father—Nemustrinus or "Lord of the Grove"—beside the stream where she washed her clothes, and loved him for the tune he played on a pipe of double reeds:

I bring no gift but this:
My chaos yielded to your genesis.
I am the shapeless clod
For you to shape into a dwarf or god.

To which she answered:

Beast, beast,
Fierce with fear,
Fear love least;
Lay your head,
Shaggy, in my arms' quiet bed. . . .
Sleep, my dear.

Because the king of her town was the tyrant Amulius, who levelled taxes as good kings bestow bounties, she was pleased for a time to share my father's hut, cook him acorn soups and lentil pies, and bear his son. But when she saw my cloven hooves and pointed ears, she cried, "I would rather nurse a goat!" and hurried back to town to pay her taxes and venerate her king. I was left to my father and his band of Fauns, who had built their camp in a grove of hickory trees, a palisade enclosing huts like stalls and gardens plump with cabbages and sweet with onion grass.

Night, like a great black hawk, had seized the camp, and the fires we built must cook our suppers and also comfort us, for Fauns are timorous in the dark, the time of ghosts, the time when ancestral spirits, the Lemures, return from the Nether Lands

to rail and reproach us because we have kept the sun.
My father, as full of years as a woodpecker tree of
holes, was at once our priest and uncrowned king.
Flanked by the elders, followed by his admiring if
uncomprehending son, he made the magic circuit of
the camp and spat out beans, nine of them, and
mumbled with each spit, "Thus I ransom me and
mine." The ghosts, it was thought, collected and ate
the beans and forgot their wrath. At least we were
spared their wails and lamentations.

Completing the circuit, he bathed his hands in
water poured from a gourd, clanged a lid on a copper cooking pot, and said, polite but stern: "Good
Folks, get you gone." At six months—six years in
human terms—I was much impressed with my father's ritual, though he, I fear, was not impressed with
me. He scolded me when I ate the largest cabbage,
ignored me when I behaved with a circumspection
beyond my months. I might have been one of the
Lemures, who manifest themselves as chills in the
air, felt, heard, but never seen (the wailing chills,
they are called). My place, I judged, was to grow
sharp horns and shaggy flanks and couple with maidens. Meanwhile, let me stick to my stall.

My father looked like a king as he faced the ghosts
—his horns had the gleam of obsidian blades. The
other Fauns, gnarled, brown, hairy creatures as old,
I thought, as the oldest oaks of the forest, squatted
on their hooves and watched with admiration and
also impatience, since they could not enjoy their sup-

per of roasted hares and myrtle berries until they had exorcised the honorable ghosts.

But scarcely had he uttered "Good Folks" than a tree trunk splintered the wall of the palisade and figures filled the opening and thrashed among us with wooden staves. "Lemures" somebody whinnied, but the staves and goatskin loin cloths belonged to shepherds. I heard the names of "Romulus" and "Wolf" —the same man, I judged, the brawniest and the youngest—and guessed him to be their king.

I scrambled to shelter in a thicket of witch grass and watched with round-eyed terror and quivering ears. Though the tumult of sandals and hooves had scattered the fires, the light of smouldering embers revealed a fearful scene: my father, lowering his head to battle the Wolf . . . a shaft like a spear . . . the clash of wood and horn . . . a reeling, stumbling figure of hair and blood. I forgot my cover and ran to his side.

"Father," I bleated. "I won't let him hit you again!"

Romulus stooped and shoveled me into the air.

Dear Faunus, I thought. He is going to eat me whole. May I give him a belly ache!

Waving me like a goatskin over his head, he delivered the high, thin wail of a hunting wolf. Then, the camp a shambles, the Fauns dazed or downed, he sprang through the broken fence and led his men, each of them carrying his own particular booty—a hempen sling, a copper pot, a roasted hare—into the forest which had disgorged them like a pack of wolves.

Proudly he clutched me against his chest—of all the stolen edibles, I was the choicest, at least the freshest—and whooped through the woods with total disregard for slumbering Lemures or real wolves or blood-sucking Striges.

I managed to jab his stomach with my hoof.

Ha! I thought. That'll teach you not to take your dinner for granted.

He gave me a hard squeeze and said between whoops, "Lie still, Goat Boy."

I wish I could boast that I retaliated with a harder kick (but Remus has taught me to tell the truth). Alas, I pretended myself into a cabbage; no, something inedible—a snug little coverlet, made from a wolfskin and rolled into a ball.

Through the trees we rushed; through antlered oaks and double-leafed elms, and feathery cypresses like Etruscan maidens dancing to soundless flutes. At last the woods turned marsh and Romulus' sandals squished in the sodden grass. I had heard my father speak of malarial country near the Tiber; I held my breath against the poisonous vapours and wished a vapour to poison Romulus.

We began to climb. Even Romulus had to pause and catch his breath. I peeped through a single eye and saw a tumble of rocks, splotches of coarse, moon-drenched grass, a summit of white stone like a single great cloud, and knew the Palatine, the fortified hill of escaped thieves and footloose shepherds.

Circular huts, thatch over clay . . . hearthfires in

31

their doors . . . the jog of the Wolf made the fires seem to dance and sway, dance and sway, and I blinked the marsh from my eyes and tried to count but lost the number at six. Sedate sheep and arrogant pigs meandered through the streets, but goats, I saw, were shut into compounds walled with piles of stones and denied the simplest means for personal cleanliness. They reeked with the various disagreeable scents of man and they fed, pathetically, on unwashed roots and rubbish.

The largest hut belonged to Romulus. We entered the low door—though Romulus stooped, he bumped my ears against the lintel—and I found myself in a windowless room with a baked earthen floor and a central fire whose smoke escaped through a hole in the roof. Romulus tossed me onto a pile of straw which I had to share with a pig, a loathly beast with crossed eyes and moist snout. I met his glare to show him who was boss, but the boss of the hut was clearly Romulus. In the light of the fire, I saw a young giant (at the time, of course, he looked overwhelmingly adult, but still the youngest in the hut). He was tall and broad, with muscular legs and with muscles taut across the bare abdomen above his loin cloth. A thin adolescent down darkened his chin, but the furrow between his eyebrows suggested ambitions beyond his years. His crow-black hair, unevenly cropped perhaps an inch from his scalp, rioted in curls.

I understood his name; I began to understand why men of every age could follow one so young. His handsome face held a wolf's cruelty, together with its strength. Older, I might have discerned a wolf's fierce tenderness; its loyalty; its tenacity in love. Older, I might have remarked the surprise and alarm when he said,

"Where's Remus?"

An aged shepherd, his long white hair bound in a fillet behind his head, rose from the fire with a look which was half a greeting and half a reprimand.

"Not back from Veii yet."

Romulus glowered. "I shouldn't have let him go without me."

"Could you have stopped him?"

Romulus grinned. "Only by breaking his skull. He'll be all right."

His men, five of them, though in the woods they had seemed a hundred, immediately began to trumpet their victory over my people.

"Hush," said the shepherd. "You sound like geese. Romulus, what are they talking about?"

"The Fauns were driving out spirits, Faustulus. Their leader said, 'Good Folks, get you gone,' and in we came! See, I have captured a kid."

"In a year he will be full grown," said Faustulus, whose face, though wrinkled like a brick shattered in a kiln, looked ageless rather than old. He was no mere shepherd, I later found, but a philosopher, a man of learning from Carthage. Wrecked in a storm near the mouth of the Tiber, he had taken shelter with herdsmen and married a skinny but resolute girl

33

named Larentia. When his bride refused to return with him to Carthage, he stayed with her people to learn their trade and, when she died of a fever, brought their foster sons, Romulus and Remus, to the Palatine and reared them as shepherds who were also princes.

"What will you do with him then? Your nocturnal games are childish, Romulus. Do they bring you closer to the throne of Alba Longa? Or to the attention of Amulius and his mercenaries?"

Romulus frowned. "Everything I do, Faustulus, brings me closer to the throne. Tonight we wrestle with Fauns. Tomorrow, soldiers. My men need practice."

Wrestle . . . practice. . . . It was a curious way to describe an invasion. Dislodging the cross-eyed pig with a surreptitious kick, I burrowed into the couch and peered between wisps of straw.

Romulus spied me in my nest. "You ask me what I will do with our captive. Eat him, Faustulus, what else? Goat flesh cooked on a spit." He clapped the back of a friend, one of the older men from the raid. "Faustulus, it seems, has lost his appetite. What about you, Celer?"

Winking at Romulus, Celer felt my arms. "Too thin, too thin. Fatten him first, eh?" His eyes were long and flat like those of an ass. His speech was thick, as if he were speaking with a mouthful of wine. I mistook him for stupid; it was the worst mistake of my life.

Romulus seemed to debate. "No," he said. "He may be thin, but I am hungry now. I'll save his ears for a belt." With a growl he hoisted me from the ground and lowered me toward the fire by the stump of my tail! I felt the flames begin to singe my ears. "I want him evenly done."

"Put him down, Romulus." The voice was young; I could not see the face.

"Brother!" cried Romulus, dropping me short of the flames but also short of the straw. I quickly reclaimed my couch from the disagreeable pig. Ensconced, I looked at the door and the newcomer, my saviour. At first it was hard to distinguish his features in the engulfment of Romulus' hug.

Released, he stood framed by the doorway like the image of a deity in a niche. Embraced by Romulus, he had appeared slight. Now, I saw him as lithe and slender; perfectly formed within his lesser dimensions. He wore a green tunic, wool, not goatskin, and caught at the waist by a leather belt with a large copper clasp. Over his shoulder hung a bow, and at his side, a quiver of arrows, their bronze nocks enwreathed with feathers to match his tunic. When I saw his hair, bound with a fillet but spilling a silken flame behind his head, I caught my breath. Picus, the woodpecker god, I thought. Who except gods and Gauls have hair like fire (and Etruscan ladies, with the help of saffron dyes)?

"Where have you *been*?" cried Romulus. "Couching princesses?"

"No," said Remus, wistful. "Listening to their father. And who is our little friend?"

"Dinner."

"Oh?" said Remus, looking down at me from his alarming height of five or six feet. I burrowed into the straw. Woodpecker gods, I feared, however beautiful, did not like Fauns, who robbed nests and scrambled bird eggs in copper skillets.

Instead of jerking my tail, he knelt and turned me around to face him. I saw the god at his throat, a boy with outstretched hand—to soothe or save. "Nameless," I prayed. "Spare me the lightning of the larger god!"

"Open your eyes," said Remus. "Please. I must see if you are hurt."

I opened my eyes. He lifted me gingerly in his arms and, fragrant with clover as if he had slept in a field, lodged me in the nook of his arm and chest and stroked the fur of my ears, smoothing it toward the tips.

"Little Faun," he said. "Don't be afraid. Tomorrow I will take you back to your people."

"Take him back!" protested Romulus. "I caught him myself."

"Fauns are not animals," said Remus. "They have lived in this forest since the time of Saturn, and we have no right to steal their children." He pointed to Romulus' bloody staff. "Or fight the fathers."

"They enjoy a fight as much as we do. We knocked them about a bit, nothing more. If I don't train my shepherds, how can they capture a city?" He grinned broadly, his white teeth glittering in the firelight. "If we don't take the city, what will we do for women?" Celer and the others—except Faustulus—roared their approval. I was later to learn that these young shepherds—thieves, wanderers, or exiles like the twins—were altogether womanless, and that Romulus had promised a house and a wife in the city for every man. Romulus winked at Celer. "My brother knows every animal in the forest. But I don't think he knows a woman from an oak tree. We will find him a girl when we take Alba Longa—a saucy wench with breasts like ripe pomegranates."

"Brother," said Remus, a slow smile curving his lips. "What do *you* know of pomegranates? You must have been gardening beyond the Palatine."

"I know!" cried Celer. "I know about them! When I served that old tyrant Amulius, I pleasured myself each night with a different girl. Had to. It was the only fun he couldn't tax. The girls I remember—"

"And the girls I imagine," sighed Remus.

"Remember, imagine," barked Romulus. "One is as bad as the other. But once we take the city! Now, Brother, tell us about your journey to Veii."

Remus took a seat on my couch and nested me in his lap. I thought about sleep. But his words were clearly important. For one thing, no one interrupted him in all of that clamorous crew. Then too there was the *way* he spoke. He had not been a boy; he had been a prince on a mission. I did not know at the

37

time why his words enthralled me; only that, warm and comfortable, I nevertheless preferred to listen instead of sleep.

As Remus described his journey, I learned why these royal twins in exile trained and plotted to seize the throne of Alba Longa from Amulius and restore their grandfather Numitor or rule in his place. Remus had gone to Veii, the Etruscan city twelve miles to the north, to ask the lucomo or king to back their cause. It was daring, indeed presumptuous for a young Latin shepherd, even a deposed prince, to seek audience with a powerful Etruscan king and ask him to war against a Latin city.

I passed into the city (said Remus) *with farmers taking shelter for the night. The palace amazed me, Romulus. Its walls were of purple stucco, and terra cotta sphinxes flanked the entrance. I told the guards that I wished to see their king; that I would speak only with him. Would they tell him that Remus, brother to Romulus and prince of Alba Longa, sought an audience.*

"Yellow Hair," one of them said. "Our king is a jolly man. I will take him word. Your boldness will make him laugh. Perhaps he will send you scraps from the kitchen."

He returned with a quizzical smile. "He will see you now."

In the banquet hall, the ceiling was painted with scenes of the Underworld. Not the gray Styx. No gray ferryman either. But the Elysium of the poets. Feasts and games and goddesses, naked except for the paint of their nipples. Winged monsters, but kindly. Strange huge cats, but pets.

The king was sharing his couch with a young woman. She was dressed like the painted goddesses above her head. Undressed, I should say. He motioned me to a couch next to him and laid his arm, heavy with amber and gold, across my shoulder. The woman smiled and passed me a bunch of grapes. Her breasts quivered like piglets with tiny red snouts.

"Remus," he said, "I have heard your story from shepherds and spies and even a prophetess. Your mother, it seems, the Vestal Novice Rhea, bore twins —you and Romulus—to the god Mars and was buried alive for breaking her vow of chastity. Her uncle, the King, ordered a shepherd to drown you in the Tiber. But he set you adrift in an osier boat. When the boat came ashore, a she-wolf suckled you in her cave and carried you to the hut of the shepherd, who reared you as his own children.

"The story is widely credited in the country, though Amulius thinks you dead—for tyrants are rarely told the truth. Every Etruscan knows that gods do indeed appear to mortals—as lovers, teachers, or friends. The god Tages, in fact, appeared to one of my own ancestors in a freshly ploughed field and gave him the books which became our holy law. I therefore greet you as the prince you call yourself. I recognize the right of Numitor, your grandfather, to

the throne usurped by his brother. But we of Veii want only peace with Alba Longa, our closest neighbor. Lead your shepherds against Amulius, if you will, and pray to Mars that the townspeople rise to help you and open the gates. Once you have seized the town and deposed the King, come to me again and we shall sign treaties of amity. Until then, let us be friends but not allies."

I looked closely into his face, the short pointed beard, black as a vulture, the arched eyebrows, the almond eyes, and saw that he would not change his mind.

"Go with this thought," he said, seeing my disappointment. "If we do not spill wine in Veii or Alba Longa, why, we shall surely banquet together in Elysium."

I took my leave and followed the basalt road through the great arched gate and returned to the Palatine.

Romulus sprang to his feet, narrowly missing my ears. "No help from Veii then. And he had the presumption to talk of the After Life! Do you know what I think, Brother? Elysium's just another name for Alba Longa—without Amulius. Alone we aren't yet strong enough to carry the place. Fifty shepherds at most, some of them old." He fingered the down on his chin, wishing, it seemed, for the ample beard—and the years—of a man. "We shall have to wait. Gather more shepherds here on the Palatine. Send scouts to feel out the mood in Alba Longa." Neither brother had ever entered the town; it was hard for princes to hide their royalty, even when dressed as shepherds. "Father Mars, let it not be long!"

He strode to the rear of the hut, where a bronze-tipped sword, green with age, lay wreathed like a holy relic with ivy leaves. He grabbed the wooden shaft. "One day soon, Holy Father, let me say to you: 'Mars, awaken!' "

"But even if we take the city," asked Remus, "will our grandfather let us rule? The throne is rightfully his."

"He is very old," said Romulus. "He will step aside —or die. When he does, we will build a temple to Mars and train an army even Etruscans fear."

"And offer asylum to birds and animals."

"Oh, Remus," chided his brother. "This is a city, not a menagerie! For once forget your animals."

"But the city can learn from the forest. Didn't I cure your fever with berries last year? A woodpecker showed them to me. And a bear brought me a fish to restore your strength."

"And the fish made me sick."

"It wasn't the fault of the bear. It was what his cub would have liked."

"Woodpeckers, bears—honestly, Remus," he smiled, "we shall have our problems ruling together. I sometimes wish that I loved you less. But let us capture the city—then we shall plan our government."

"Now it is late," said Faustulus. "Almost cockcrow

time. Even princes need their sleep." He placed his hand lovingly on Remus' shoulder.

Remus grasped the hand. "Good Father," he said, "we talk of palaces. But huts, I think, may hold more love." Then he rose to his feet and kissed Romulus soundly on the cheek. Yes, kissed him, a man kissing a man! Why not a soft, cuddlesome Faun who lay at his feet like a good little lamb?

Never mind. He gathered me in his arms and left the hut. I could have walked, of course. I had crawled at a month; walked at two. But I did not want to lose my ride. Stumbling with his burden (not that I was fat; still, six months of Faun—!), he descended the rocky path toward the Tiber, which looped like an adder in the light of the stars and swelled in places as if digesting a meal. At the foot of the Palatine we entered the mouth of a cave where a small fire burned on a raised clay hearth. Remus stirred the coals.

"I hate the dark," he said. "It seems to whisper with spirits. People like my mother. If I could only believe the Etruscans. . . ."

My poor small mind, strained to its limit by talk of exile, revolt, revenge, could not encompass thoughts of the After Life. I looked for a place to sleep. Earthen floor soft with rushes and clover . . . pallet of clean white wool. . . . I would dream, I knew, as soon as I touched the ground. Except for the dog asleep by the fire. Large, uncouth, and odoriferous. A watchdog, no doubt, forgetting to watch. Well, I had cowed a pig with a well-aimed kick. Just let that mangy dog. . . .

She was not a dog.

She was a wolf.

Yellowing fur matted with age, she rose gigantically on her haunches and confronted us with bared fangs. I clung to Remus' neck.

"Lie still, little Faun," he laughed as he disengaged me and placed me on the pallet. "This is Luperca, my foster mother. She's trying to smile! It was she who found Romulus and me on the bank of the Tiber and brought us to her lair. Then to Faustulus and Larentia. She is very old now. Sometimes she wanders in the woods—I think she visits a friend—but at night she shares my cave and my supper."

He knelt beside her and stroked her black-rimmed ears. Remembering, I can see nobility in the scene, the boy with slender hands and hair as yellow as sunflowers, the aged wolf who had suckled him in her cave. At the time, however, I saw a flea-bitten and unmannerly beast who threatened to steal my new friend's attention from me.

"My name is Sylvan," I snapped.

"I didn't know you could talk," he laughed, settling beside me on the pallet.

"Nobody asked me."

"Well, we shall have a long talk tomorrow."

"I want to talk *now*." I really wanted to sleep, but we have a phrase in the woods, "Stubborn as a Faun."

"All right, Sylvan. Tell me about your family."

"Sixteen brothers, sixty uncles, ninety-nine cousins——"

"Sylvan, I must teach you how to add."

"Oh, very well, I do have a father. Romulus hit him."

"That was wrong of Romulus."

"He's all right, I expect. He has a hard head. I had a mother once, but she ran off to Alba Longa because she disliked my horns."

"*I* like them," he said.

"I thought you would."

"And when we take the city, Fauns will be as welcome as men."

"Truly?"

"Have you seen the city?" he asked, and before I could tell him yes, that an old Faun had carried me to the walls and pointed, "That is where your mother ran off to," he continued, "It is very small, really just a town. But its houses are white and clean, and its temple to Vesta is as pure as—as my mother's heart. It is now an unhappy place. Amulius is a harsh ruler. He murdered my mother, Sylvan. He laughed when she told him that Mars was my father. 'You have broken your vow,' he said, and buried her alive in the ground. Faustulus had a friend who saw her before she died. Just a girl, really. Bewildered but proud. She looked at Amulius with her large black eyes and said: 'Mars is my husband and he will protect my sons.'

44

"Everyone believed her except Amulius. You see now why I hate him. And I have other reasons. He sends his hunters into the woods to kill the bears and the wolves. He taxes the vintners a third of their wine and the shepherds a fourth of their sheep. What do they get in return? The protection of soldiers—when they are not killing animals or stealing sheep. But Sylvan, forgive me. I am keeping you awake with problems beyond your months. Tomorrow I will take you home."

"Remus," I said.

"Yes, little Faun?"

"I already am."

II

I did not count the months, twelve of them, gliding as imperceptibly as the Tiber after its burden of snow, before the summer has shrunken it into a stream. Season succeeded season, but I, so I thought, could linger in spring, eternally child to Remus' man.

If I did not count the months, I had to count the inches until I found myself as tall and strong as the god who had rescued me from the fire, and something better than child: his equal and friend. I was proud of my curving horns, my trim, triangular ears. I looked at my face in the Tiber and I was proud for *him*. I did not want to affront him with ugliness, not having learned, as yet, that Remus only loved faces that figured souls. My skin was the bronze of Etruscan shields. I carried my ears like banners of silken fur. I spruced my tail with a hazel branch and kept it free from thorns. ("Faunus," I prayed, "let me remain a sapling as long as Remus, and not, like my father, gnarl into age." It was an impious prayer, the kind which is answered to spite us for our presumption.)

"Remus," I liked to say. "Shall we wench in the woods tonight?"

It was one of our jokes. The towns, so we thought, held all of the girls. "Alba Longa!" became our mutual sigh. Still, it was my happy time. Secretly, I did not want it to end with a war and a throne for my friend. He had said that a hut could hold more love than a town. I would have said a cave (even with Luperca). To talk about hunting the hare and the wild boar, but never the bear, or building temples and making laws—the subjects he liked—to talk about raising a palisade or searching for Dryads—the subjects I liked . . . well, could I ask for a greener life?

"You should visit your father," he said as he stirred the coals on the first anniversary of my rescue from that other fire.

"Should I? He won't even have missed me."

"Sylvan, it's been a year. Twelve to you! Give him

a chance." To Remus, a family tie endured at least until death. Quarrels, indifferences—these might loosen but only gods could part.

My grandfather's friends had built a new camp with high walls and sharp stakes. "Romulus-proof," I laughed, though scared to the tips of my hooves. Happily, we did not have to enter the place. I saw an ancient Faun in front of the gate and knew him by the scar which Romulus' staff had left between his horns; and by his ears, longish, convoluted like the throat of a trumpet shell.

"It is well with you?" he asked, knowing me in return, ignoring Remus.

"Yes," I said, hopeful, I think, of a hug, a clasp of hands, a simple touch. For Remus—Romulus too—had taught me that men could show affection without becoming women.

"Good," he said. "I thought they might have killed you." He left us without a word or a backward look. The gate, like a row of prodigious teeth, did not invite visitors.

"Never mind," said Remus. "I am your family now."

"It's just that we have such a little time—the Fauns, I mean. Hardly time to love. My father is almost twenty. That's as old as we get. And he hasn't learned a thing."

"You have, Sylvan."

"Have I? I guess I got an early start."

"See that you don't forget. I'll race you to the cave. The loser has to fix Luperca's dinner."

He let me win.

The Palatine Hill was mushroomed now with huts, and that of Romulus was the roundest and largest in the multitude. Sabine shepherds from the neighboring hill, the Quirinal, had joined their lot with the Wolf; and much against Remus' will, thieves and murderers from the forest, sullen men, as mixed as a band of slaves from the infamous galleys of Carthage.

"Murderers make good soldiers," Romulus argued. "They've nothing to lose, and women and treasure to gain."

As shepherds, of course, the brothers must care for sheep and cattle, leading from pasture to pasture below the Palatine, guarding from wolf and bear, and making sacrifice to the Pales, the shepherd gods, and the lady of nursing mothers, the gentle Rumina. The herds they tended belonged to a wealthy Alba Longan, Marcus, a friend to Amulius and after him the richest man in the town. It was his overseer, a plump, drowsy dormouse of a man, Balbus by name, who brought us word of increasing tyrannies.

"The King has doubled the taxes," he drawled, sleepily rubbing his eyes. "What is more, his soldiers are out of control! Today they insult a Vestal in the streets. Tomorrow, behead a boy for petty theft. I tell you, Faustulus, my master serves a tyrant."

"And the people," inquired Romulus, an edge of bronze to his voice. "Why do they take such treatment?"

"The people are cowed." He blinked and wrinkled his nose. I looked for a tail. "Amulius' soldiers number a thousand—trained to kill, and paid with the land and cattle and armor"—there was no coinage yet in Latium—"stolen from those they rob. Nobody likes the soldiers. The soldiers don't even like each other. Etruscans refuse to eat with Carthaginians. Greeks quote Homer and keep to themselves. But what can citizens do without a leader?"

Romulus left his herds in the care of sheep dogs and drilled his men mercilessly in the midday sun or the torrential rains of Jupiter; he taught them to climb cliffs like city walls or move with the stealth of wolves. On the hill called Aventine, Remus taught them to whittle bows from hickory limbs and feather their arrows for speed and accuracy. Even I had my place. Men were used to fighting with bows and swords, but in the press of battle such weapons were often enemies instead of allies. I taught them how to butt and kick, sidestep, parry, and lunge. True, they lacked my natural weaponry.

"Boots are as hard as hooves," I said. "A hornless head can be a battering ram."

But even warriors must have a rest; even shepherds, forget their herds at times. Thus, my Adventure with Remus. I will not call it fun. It began because I found him close to tears. I knew the look (whenever he thought about his mother, buried in her pit). I must jolly him out of his mood.

I crept upon him like a stealthy old Faun upon a

virgin; I seized him around his waist and rolled him in the grass. My weakness when we wrestled was my tail; my comeliest appurtenance, downier than the breast of a quail, but purely decorative; in battle, a distinct liability. Of course he always aimed for the tail. He liked to seize and jerk until I begged for mercy before he shredded the fur or wrenched the shape. For once, I took him by surprise. I sat on his chest and pressed his arms against the grassy ground.

"Rumina be witness," I said, for her sacred fig tree flourished above our heads, a leafy shrine.

"Enough," he gasped. "Let me up!"

"Won't trick me?"

"Won't."

He climbed gingerly to his feet and made a show of testing muscle and bone before he stood at his full height.

"Next time," he smiled, "I'll jerk out your tail by the roots!" But the tears were not exorcised.

"Sylvan," he sighed. "My bees are dying."

He had found the bees exposed in a hollow log, stunned them with smoke, and removed them carefully to a hole in the fig tree, safe from hungry bears and thievish shepherds. At first they had seemed to thrive and Remus had been as proud as a Faun with a new cabbage patch. He had not even borrowed their honey—"They need it themselves." But now. . . .

"Look," he said, drawing me to the tree, a giant of its kind, which lifted its broad rough leaves to a height of forty feet. "The bees are very sick."

I stood beside him, hand on his shoulder, and peered into the leaves. The bees were removing their dead instead of discharging nectar or repairing the hive. Two of them, overwhelmed by the weight of a fallen comrade, fell to the ground at my feet and fluttered helplessly in the grass.

"They look beyond our help," I said. "But there are other hives, Remus. There will be no lack of honey."

"But I am fond of *these*," he protested, turning to face me. "They are my friends, Sylvan. Not once have they stung us."

"Speak for yourself," I started to say, nursing my extremities, but he looked so troubled, so young and defenseless, that I bit back my words and held back my tears. (Fauns make a show of carelessness; perhaps my love for Remus had made me soft. Still, I was not ashamed.) In the year I had known him he had hardly changed. His face did not even hint a beard. Who could explain how this blond, green-eyed boy, so different from dark Romulus, had sprung from a dusky Latin mother? Only Mars knew the answer. Yet Rhea, the gentle yet stubborn Novice, and not the warlike Mars, seemed much more truly his parent.

"Wait," I said. "Fauns like honey and sometimes keep bees. My father will know what to do."

We went to find him in his new camp to the south of the Aventine. Though unencumbered with clothes, I hardly managed to keep pace with Remus in his tunic and sandals. He skimmed through the woods as if he had borrowed wings from his woodpecker god; in fact he had sewn his tunic with feathers from the bird.

"Remus, take pity," I gasped. "I expect you to rise through the treetops!"

"Remember, a woodpecker fed me when I was small."

"And gave you his wings, though not, thank Faunus, his disposition."

In the deepest part of the woods, the trees were as old as Saturn and the Golden Age. What they had seen had left them tired—bowed, twisted, and sagging—but still august. Oak was·the oldest tree, but ilex too, and gray-barked beech mixed sunlight and shadow into a mist of limbs. Blue-eyed owls hooted their wise-sounding inanities, and magpies, birds of good omen, chattered in hidden eyries. A woodpecker burned his small red flame against the conflagration of the forest, and Remus pointed to him excitedly. "It was one like that who fed me berries."

"Yes, I know, and a mangy . . . and Luperca gave you suck."

"And what are *they?*" he asked.

Among the trees, a pool as round as a Cyclops' eye. . . . Boys, not human . . . inhumanly beautiful.

"Fonti, fountain spirits."

"They don't even see us, do they?"

"They see everything. Just let a girl fall in love with them. Here's a poem I made up about them. Well, a sort of poem. Prosy, don't you see. I haven't had time to polish." I composed in fact as I spoke:

"Blue boys; kingfisher-blue hair; eyes like lapis lazuli drowned in the sea; as blue, as pure, as cold. Blue boys frolicking in the silver foam. *Green girls, love them to your despair.* 'Blue Boys!' Kingfisher-quick they twinkle under the foam; after them, laughter rippling into silver despair for her who loves a blue boy with heart of foam, silverly twinkling; quicksilvered air. *Green girl, comb your hair.*"

"I like the poem but I don't like them," he said.
"Why not?"
"Perfection makes me shiver."
"What they need is an—eccentricity?"
"Exactly."
"What would suit?"
"Hooves. And a silken tail."
Suddenly I thought: Thank Jupiter, Remus is imperfect—he loves an imperfection named Sylvan.

At the palisade, I bleated to signify my wish to speak with one of the Fauns. The gate opened on oiled leather hinges. Momentarily, I had the image of a huge, toothless mouth. A Faun, knotty and mottled like the underside of a rock, appeared in place of a tongue.

"It is Sylvan," I said. "Will you tell my father Nemustrinus that I wish to see him?"

Suspicious and uncommunicative, ears aquiver, he turned in his tracks to engage in a consultation punctuated by bleats, whinnies, and telling silences. Miraculously my father materialized in the gate.

"Sylvan," he said, somber and toneless. "You want me?"

"Yes, Father, this is Remus. Remember?"

"Do you think I have lost my memory as well as my silk?"

"We need your help. Remus' bees are dying. We hoped you could help us save them. The hive is well situated. But a sickness has taken them. They are carrying off their dead."

He thought; at least, I assumed a thought behind his unreadable wooden mask of a face. "You must find a Dryad then."

"A Dryad, Father?"

"Yes. They speak to the bees. They know the cures."

"But Dryads are rare in these parts. I have never seen one."

"I have," he said, his voice swelling with pride. "Her hair was the colour of oak leaves gilded with sun. Her skin, like milk. . . ." He paused to remember. The memory, it seemed, was too exquisite to share. Or shameful? Perhaps she had repulsed him. "But I will tell you where to look. Two miles to the south of this camp, there is a circle of oaks. Some say Saturn planted them. At any rate, one is inhabited by a Dryad. Which I cannot remember. It was such an age ago—You must hide in the bushes besides the altar and watch the bees. In the tree where the most of them light you will find your Dryad. Taking her nectar, you see. But tell me, Sylvan, why are these bees so important? Let them die. Find another hive."

"They are our friends," said Remus. "We like to hear them work outside our cave. Now they are almost silent."

"Friends, you call them? Let me look at you, boy. Ah, the old eyes in the young face. Your hair is ripe barley, but your heart knew Saturn. In the old time, there was love in the forest. There were silver bells. Or so the records say. A scrawl on a stone, a picture, an image of clay—always they tell of love. Fauns, men, and animals living in harmony." He turned to me.

"Look after him, Sylvan. Help him to find his Dryad. Help him always. He is one who is marked to be hurt."

The gate closed in our face.

"Sylvan," said Remus, seeing my pain. "He's an old man. He didn't mean to be abrupt with you."

My pain was not for my father's indifference; it was for his prediction.

"Let's find your Dryad," I said.

We found the circle of oaks; on the crumbling altar, a wreath of violets lay like a cry to the past. Fingers of sunlight touched the ruinous stones, the plants overrunning them, white narcissi with red-rimmed coronas, spiny-leafed acanthuses, and jonquils, yellow as if the sunlight had flowered into petals, yellow as Remus' hair.

"Such a riot of flowers," said Remus. "It is surely a sacred place. And the violets—someone still worships here."

"And here. A kind of temple, I think."

It was one of those forest shrines which seem to be grown instead of built. An arbor of hickory boughs —stakes remembering trees—had been curved and curled into a leafy dome. Wild roses for roof (pink and white, stars in a green night); roseate mist above the door. Enter the fragrant dusk: stone altar inscribed with the name of a god—Vaticanus. Instead of an image, a cradle of tortoise shell on wooden rockers.

"Vaticanus! The god you wear around your neck. But he belongs to the nursery, not the forest."

"He belongs wherever there are babies. Somebody in these parts must be a parent. See? There are more violets. In the cradle."

"Remus, you have your mystical look. Are you ready to meditate? If you are, I'm leaving."

"No," he laughed. "It's just that I feel as if I were coming home. I've been here before."

"Not since I came to live with you."

"There was the time before you came."

"Oh, that," I said. "That doesn't count. Are you forgetting the bees? Hide now, worship later." I dragged him into concealment behind the stones of the altar. "You know," I scolded, "if you go about mooning like that, a wolf will get you yet. In spite of Luperca."

A swarm of bees approached the circle of oaks; poised in the air like a tawny cloud; funneled into a welter of greenery. They had chosen the tallest oak. "Twenty feet or so broad," I muttered. "Room for a whole family. Remus, let's go."

"No," he whispered. "Your father said to watch where the *most* bees go."

We waited, I fretfully, since a moment to a man is twelve to a Faun. Soon I grew sleepy and, using Remus' back for a pillow, slept until he yanked my tail.

"Three swarms have entered that tree and left again! No other tree has attracted so many. That must be the one."

We broke our cover and walked to the tallest tree.

"But how do we get inside?" asked Remus, staring at the huge, impervious trunk, its climbable limbs impossibly out of our reach. "The bees flew down through the branches way at the top." We circled the base, prodding among the roots and dislodging a turquoise lizard which flickered over my hoof and disappeared among the altar stones.

Thoughtful, Remus stared after him. "Do you think he knows something we don't?" A field mouse, forgetting flight, preened his whiskers on the tallest stone. A honey bee surged from a shaken jonquil cup.

"Sylvan," he called. "I think we've found it!" He knelt among the stones. "This one isn't a stone, it's a——"

"Cleverly disguised door."

"A ladder," he beamed. "I'll go first. Careful you don't crush a jonquil."

"But we didn't knock," I wailed, thinking of adders and angry girls; foreseeing, dimly, *change*. Remus was deaf when he set his mind to a task. Muttering to assorted lizards and mice, placating possible adders, I followed him into the earth.

The walls had been cleaned of roots and rocks, but the tunnel was long and the blackness seemed to seethe with coils and fangs. I suspected an adder with every loop or bend.

At last we began to climb; the scent of wood revealed the place—the trunk; we hoped, the house. A light shone roundly above our heads. The ladder yielded to wooden rungs, carved inside of the trunk like spiral stairs.

"We've found it," he cried, joyfully yanking my tail. "We have found her house!"

"I hope she is more accessible than her house," I managed to puff. *If you were half as solicitous about my tail as about those freeloading bees—*

I thought of "Dryad" with every step and pictured a woman as gnarled as a trunk and as gray as moss. *Hoary,* that was the word. (*Whorey*?)

"Remus," I whispered. "You know they aren't all young. They die of old age like humans, only it takes them longer. Toward the end, they get to be hags."

"This one is young." I had seen him scratching pictures on the walls of our cave, Rumina and other goddesses. He invariably drew them as youthful mothers, high of breast and full of face, the image of Woman in his own young heart.

"She may have lost her teeth, and her breath will smell of toadstools, the poisonous kind, and her breasts will be wizened nubs. Raisins without any juice. Did you hear that, Remus? *Raisins without any juice.*"

"Hush!"

We found ourselves in a circular room the size of Romulus' hut. House, not hut, said the furnishings. Small round windows admitted the sun to mingle shadow with light; dusk with dawn. Hard contours melted into mist; magic held the place. Ivy grew on the walls, a living tapestry, and potted poppies disported like fledgling cabbages. A minikin pool, like a lily pad with a rim, frolicked with tadpoles and crimson fish.

"Why, it's good enough to eat!"

"What, Sylvan?"

"The whole room. It's one big garden—fish for dessert. And here's the table. Wouldn't you know? wooden vines on the legs. Feet like acorns!"

"Citrus wood from Carthage," he said. "I saw one like it in Veii. Here's the same wood in a chair. But its feet are those of a lion."

"Ready to go foraging."

"Sylvan, put that poppy back!"

"I was only going to eat *one*. We've had such a trying search."

"We're guests," he said.

I replaced the pot minus its poppy. "The stairs continue. There must be a second floor above our heads. A kitchen, I expect." •

"And a couch. I'll call her. She mustn't think we are thieves."

"Wait. I hear some steps."

Unhurried yet purposeful, footsteps descended the stairs; a pair of sandals preceded the legs of a young woman, and a tunic girdling a full but shapely waist, and breasts which were melons instead of raisins, and then a face like that of Remus' dream. We saw her in stages; the whole exceeded the parts; the whole was a Dryad and also a Woman. She was small, I grant, but edibles flourished in every region and made a garden tastier than her house.

Suddenly I thought of walls. Her hair fell long and loosely over her shoulders, obsidian-black in the shadows, jade in the sun with plentiful lodes of gold. Her mouth was pink, small, and coralline; her skin, the white of a seashell sunned on a beach but not yet cracked or marred. A green linen robe, embroidered with brown shields, rippled to sandaled feet. Ripe waist, melons, gardens—soft things. Obsidian, jade, coral, shell, shield—hard things. Beauty was armor guarding her softnesses. Or was the softness merely deceit; armor, all?

She chose her words as I might choose the stones for my sling. She chose to wound.

"You have violated my house. You there. Acorn Eater. Your clumsy hooves disturbed my sleep. May Janus, the Door God, molt your hair. And"—to Remus—"who are you? Your face is hidden in the shadows."

Stubbornly, he did not step into the sun. We were wrong but she was rude.

"As for violating your house, we couldn't be sure it *was* a house until we found this room. Then we forgot ourselves in its beauty." He paused. "We have come to ask a favour."

"A favour?" she cried. "I can guess the one you mean."

She fixed her glare on me. "You are the worst, you Fauns. Did it never occur to you to cover your loins? At least your friend has the decency to wear a tunic."

"If you notice my nakedness," I snapped, "perhaps it is because you admire it. Dryads need men, and Fauns need women. Why should they not be friends?"

"I have banqueted with a king. Shall I frolic with strangers who blunder in from the woods—a Faun and a . . . a shepherd?"

"We came to ask you about our bees," insisted Remus. His plea would have melted a Gorgon's heart. "They are dying and we want you to help us heal them."

Silent, she scrutinized him, trying no doubt to distinguish his features in the shadowy light. She could not see the weave of his feathered tunic, the god he wore at his throat; the prince's mein. She saw a shepherd companioned by a Faun.

He moved toward her. Ah, I thought. At last she will see his face, the face of the woodpecker god. She raised a cautioning hand. Accustomed to being liked, he misunderstood; he mistook her gesture for a sign of peace and clasped the hand.

Then, incredibly, unpredictably even to me, who loved him above all men, above the gods, he took her in his arms and kissed her clumsily on her small pink lips. Quick as an adder her hand shot from her waist—I saw the onyx blade—and raked him down his side.

With a cry he withdrew, staring not at his bloodstreaked side but at her, and not with anger but shame at his own affront. I struck the knife from her hand and pinioned her with my arms. She struggled; I rammed a knee in her back.

"Lie still," I snapped. "You hurt my friend. Remus, kiss her again."

"Let her go," he said.

"But Remus, she cut you even through your tunic. I can see the blood. She deserves what she feared."

"Sylvan, let her go," he said, a small boy, baffled, defeated, not to be disobeyed. I released her. She stared at the bloody rent.

"Please," he said to her. "My bees are dying. Tell me what to do for them."

She took his hand and led him under a window—the light kindled his face into a grave, luminous sunflower—and dabbed the blood with the sash from her own waist.

"Burn a pinch of galbanum under the hive and carry them clusters of raisins in leaves of thyme. They will multiply and grow strong again." She seemed to be hypnotized by his face. "I have never seen such hair. Except once. Like flax, but soft as the silken strands in a spider web. You are just a boy. At first I thought you were like the rest."

"I am," he said. "I came to ask you about my bees, but I forgot them. You made me think of grass and flowers in the warm sun. I am like the rest. I wanted to lie with you."

"But you told your friend to release me. Why weren't you angry when I wounded you?"

"I was. With myself."

"Listen! The bees are bringing me honey. My little friends from the forest. Your friends too."

Like round-built merchant ships with precious oils, they invaded the room and disgorged their nectar into an agate cup. They lit on her outstretched arms and made a nest of her hair.

"Their lives are brief and perfect. Six weeks perhaps. They do their work; they know the great blue sky like the cradling wing of a god; they sleep with the first frost. I have sometimes envied them."

"But why?" he asked. "I have heard that a Dryad may live a hundred years or more."

She smiled the archaic smile of Sibyls and goddesses. "I am four hundred and eighty-seven years old."

"I took you for twenty-five," he gasped. "An older woman, yes, but beautiful, wordly. Not——"

"Ancient? I could tell you of gods who come to Earth."

"My father was such a god."

I am drunk from the nectar, I thought. I must clear my head.

"Remus," I said, "I will wait by the pile of stones."

"I know," she said. "The Holy Father Mars." I might have been a tadpole dreaming of frog or a flower in one of her pots. She did not ignore me; she had forgotten me. "I knew you from your flaxen hair, and the god at your throat. Fair Hair."

"The god?"

"You."

"You speak it like a name."

"You have another. The Bird of Fire."

I backed down the stairs. . . .

MELLONIA

At first I took them for thieves.

In my dream, a coverlet of snow, warm and companionable, had settled over the woods. I discarded my tunic, my accumulation of years and sorrows, and opened my arms to catch the gentling flakes. It seemed to me that a goddess had answered my prayer—Venus, the lady of love, who releases from love; or gray-eyed Rumina, a friend at partings as well as beginnings. She had sent me the snow as a winding sheet.

Then, the thud of feet, the tremulous floor beneath my couch.

Invasion!

A Faun, of course. No one else could have found my hidden door; finding, presumed to invade the house of a Dryad and queen. At least he was not odorous. I could not see the face of his friend. His figure was young; his words were soft and courteous. A shepherd but not unlettered, I thought. But he runs with a Faun. He has learned his pretty speeches from a Faun. Does he play the same tricks? When he seized my hand and kissed me on the mouth, I was quick with my knife. I have had to be quick.

The hurt in his face will haunt me to the Styx. His beauty was from the gods. No one had given him his innocence; it was his purple, it was his princeliness. I had wounded him; like a rusty blade, I had tried to tarnish him with my age, suspicion, seclusion. . . .

"Remus," I said, "prince of Alba Longa. Fair Hair. Bird of Fire. Can you climb the stairs? I have herbs in a room above your head. Your wound is slight—believe me, I did not strike to kill—but even a scratch may invite a demon."

"Sylvan tends my wounds."

"Sylvan is gone."

"But he didn't say goodbye!"

"He tried. He promised to wait for you among the stones."

"Oh, then he's all right. I thought you might have hurt him too." He paused; his eyes were windows into his soul: I saw a clean, sunny room with a bow hung on the wall and a scroll unwound on the couch. There were no shadows. "Those names you called me. . . ." A little boy, he yielded himself into my hands. . . . *A little boy from an osier boat in the reeds.*

"I was your first mother in the woods."

"Not Luperca?"

"Luperca too. It was she who brought you milk."

"She still comes here, doesn't she? Till now, I thought she had a mate in the woods."

"She's much too old for a mate. Actually, she's been coming here from the first."

"And you were my mother too. . . ."

"It was I who cradled you in this very house. I did not know your name at the time. I called you Fair Hair to distinguish you from your dark brother. Also, I called you the Bird of Fire and him the Little Wolf."

"What is *your* name? I hope you haven't as many as I have."

"Mellonia."

"The Lady of the Bees. But you need a special name because of your green hair and your pointed ears and your tunic embroidered with acorns. Green-O-the-Woods. Do you like it?"

"Aeneas might have given me such a name. Not Ascanius. His mind never ran to poetry. He was a warrior, though gentle in his way."

"But Ascanius was my own ancestor! He is very famous in Alba Longa. He built the first building. It's still there, a shrine to his father's Lar."

"Then, there was justice. The builder remembered Troy."

"Not any more. Not under Amulius. He killed my mother."

"I saw her before she died."

"Saw her? How was she beautiful?"

I envied his certainties. He seemed to speak of a world which had died with Troy. Gods loved mortals. Valor belonged irrevocably to princes, beauty to princesses.

"Like a young fir tree. They could not break her pride. You have had four mothers, in all. I am the second. Here, sit on my couch. I will find the herb for your wound. Tincture of wintergreen. It soothes and heals."

"You don't look like a mother," he said. "You don't look at *all* like a mother. Larentia was old and skinny long before she died. I loved her, but she always smelled like wool. As if she had just been unfolded from a chest. You smell of violets. Like the ones you left in the temple and at the altar. Your hand is a sunbeam tickling down my side."

"That is the wintergreen starting to heal. You saw my little offerings to Vaticanus and Rumina?"

"If I were a god I would give you your wish."

"Aren't you?"

"No," he said. "Romulus says we're each of us half a god because of Mars, our father. I don't think so. I think godhead has to be earned, even half. What would you ask if I were a whole god, though?"

"To be all young or all old."

"Why not the best of both—wintergreen? It heals, you just told me so."

"I am not a plant," I smiled, "in spite of my tree and my green blood."

"Sylvan said your houseplace was a garden. You make me think of an orchard behind a fence."

"Please," I said, disarmed by the stare of his green unblinking eyes. Every youngness was in them . . . fledgling . . . sapling . . . bear cub . . . boy. "Stop pounding the gate."

"One last knock," he smiled before he turned his exacting attention to the room; fingered the linen coverlet on the couch; peered in the chest from which I drew the herb; but always returned to me, as if to associate me with my things.

"A poor room," I shrugged. "My treasures are in the houseplace or kitchen. Here, I sleep. It is enough."

"The couch is a treasure," he noted, kneeling to study the legs. "Why, its feet are the paws of a lion. And it looks as soft as grass."

"There were once lions in the forest. They were friends with my son, Cuckoo."

"And the couch? Where did you get it?"

"I carved the legs myself. Stretched a sheepskin across the frame. Stuffed the cushions with moss. A trifle, though comfortable. Perhaps you would like to examine my scrolls. There, in the chest beside the stairs. Notice the holes like slots, each of them filled with a scroll. Homer—his view of the Trojan War is not entirely accurate. He was a Greek. The Egyptian Book of the Dead. A Cretan manuscript about the last Minotaur."

"My foster father sometimes quoted Homer to me. But the couch isn't a trifle. It feels quite—commodious."

"And there are my household gods." In niches above his head stood three small images: Venus in gold, Rumina in marble, Vaticanus in bronze. Unlike Dryads, unlike Etruscans and Greeks, the Alba Longans do not represent their gods as men and women, Mars is a spear, Vesta a hearth fire, Venus a myrtle flower, Vaticanus a cradle, Rumina a cylix of milk.

But Remus guessed the names. "The gold one is surely Venus. She looks so giving." A reasonable guess. She was nude and voluptuous. "And the lady in marble. Dressed simply in homespun, in spite of the rich stone. A shepherdess, I would say. Rumina?"

"Yes."

"And the boy with wheat in his hand—he matches the god I wear around my throat. Vaticanus."

"He watched over you in my tortoise shell. Whispered a song into the ear of a friend of mine."

"Was I a good baby? Or did I squall and blubber?"

"I don't recall that you ever blubbered. Romulus either, though he squalled to get what he wanted."

"Now he shouts. It still works. Except he doesn't shout at me because he doesn't have to. I love him, you see. But you haven't told me if I was good."

"As good as my own son, Cuckoo."

"I wish I had known Cuckoo. I like children. It's hard to remember myself as a child, though. I seem to have always been grown. I guess I have come to the age when one takes stock."

Strange, his thinking of Cuckoo as always a child. Perhaps he had read my thought.

"Do you know," he said, "I was a sort of father once."

"Well, it isn't surprising. Virginity isn't a virtue in men. Or women either, so I am told by my aunt."

"I don't mean *that*," he said wistfully, "though I wish it were so. I would like to be a real father. But this was a child I rescued from my brother. You saw him. He's grown up now." His smile was a sunburst. "Don't you think I made a good parent?"

"The Faun?" I cried.

A shadow eclipsed the sun. "What's wrong with Sylvan?"

"Nothing," I shrugged. "For a Faun, he appeared to be remarkably clean."

"For a Faun? What do you mean?"

A queen, I was not accustomed to accusations in my own house, particularly when I had spoken with haste and spite.

"Well," I groped, "they don't bathe, they tell disgraceful lies, they try to lure you with pretty speeches—"

"They? Do you think they're all the same?"

"Some are worse than others. It was a Faun who killed Aeneas."

"I have heard the story," he said. "But it might just as well have been a man—or a Dryad."

Abruptly I saw my old heart in all of its blotches and wrinkles. My young face was a lie. It did not reveal my handiwork through the years. I had filled a Pandora's Box with grievances.

"Yes," I said slowly, "it might have been. As a matter of fact, it was a Dryad—queen before me—who paid him to kill Aeneas. Tell me about Fauns. Tell me about your friend."

"Well, in the Golden Age, Fauns patrolled the forests and rescued travelers from wolves and storms. If you needed their help, you listened for the tinkle of bells and cried in a loud voice, "Silver Bells, bring me your valiant hooves!" Sylvan is my Silver Bells. I love him most in the world along with my brother.

And it's much more fun to be with him than Romulus. He doesn't expect me always to talk about battles. You might say we ruminate together. What is more, I can tell him things and he never judges."

"It is hard," I said, "to grow old without judging. But in the end, I think, one reserves the harshest judgment for oneself."

"Why do you keep pretending to be an old woman? I don't feel at all as if you were my mother. An older woman, yes, as I said. But lovely and enigmatic and —well, you make me feel as if I want to explore."

"We have much to explore together, you and I. All that has happened since you were a babe in arms."

"You want to put me back into somebody's arms. That's fine, but please, not a mother's. I'm practically middle-aged. *Eighteen*."

"I will sing you a Dryad song."

"Not a nursery song, mind you."

"A season song."

"Oh, very well."

I could see that he would not make an attentive audience. His mind was on explorations. I must sing briefly and well to make my point:

A Dryad's Lament

Old as the dust of trampled Babylon,
She sleeps within that shrunken tower, her tree,
And sleeping waits for one immortal gift,
Mortality.

Not January's brittle-fingered frost,
Nor March, abrupt with rowdy blossoming,
Now August, opulent with bursted grape
And whirr of wing

Shall quicken her. But when October lies
In amber dissolution on the land,
She wakes and, amorous of the dying leaves,
Uplifts her hand:

The leaves will understand.

"It's very tender and sad. But that's what I mean.
Sleep . . . Old Age. That's not you."

"Can you read my heart?"

"Better than you can read mine."

"And what do you see?"

"A green tree with some moss on its limbs. Green,
I say. Leaves as well as wood. The moss only came
because it was allowed."

Carefully I withdrew the hand which he had recaptured, quite unconsciously I think, in the pursuit of
his metaphor.

"Perhaps——"

"You see!" he cried. "You won't even let me touch
you. I must be ill-favored as Celer says. Sometimes I
envy Sylvan his horns and silky tail. I have so much
less to commend me. If only I had a tail——" I hid my
smile in the shadows. A young god lamenting divin-

ity! But then, there had been no women to mirror his beauty to him.

I took his face between my hands. "Ill-favored, my dear? What a foolish thing to say! From the time you were one month old——"

"Then you think it's wrong," he said, jerking his head from between my hands.

"What?"

"What comes after the first embrace. I can tell. You expect me to bring you my cares like a little child. You want to comfort me. They made my mother a Novice, but she knew better. She had her way with a god, and she was right."

"But she was seventeen. You say I want to comfort you. True. As the she-bear comforts her cub——"

"I like bears, but I am not a cub and I don't particularly want an additional mother, with or without fur. I seem to have had my share, including a wolf."

"A dear friend then——"

"I have Sylvan. The dearest. I want a beloved."

"And you shall find her. A girl your own age."

"I detest girls. They giggle and simper and talk about gowns and trinkets."

"What do you know about girls? I thought there were only men on the Palatine."

"Celer has told me. I grew up fast, almost like Sylvan. I have had no time for such foolishness. What I want is a woman of years and experience."

"And what experiences should she have had?"

"She should have had two lovers and borne a son to the first. She should be a queen who has lost her subjects but not her looks. She should speak eloquently on such matters as love, death, and the After Life. Also, she should know when to remain silent."

"Very well," I smiled. "I shall try to talk eloquently about love. Love to me was Aeneas. Do you know how the halcyon builds his nest on the sea, and the Tritons silence the waters until his mate can hatch her eggs? I had been taught by women—mother, aunts, the queen who bribed the Faun to stab Aeneas. He had been taught by wars. But it was he who understood peace. What shall I say of him? He made me unafraid."

"Tell me about Ascanius."

"There was more variety in him, less consistency. Good and bad mingled like jonquils and bindweed. He did a hateful thing. He killed my dearest friend, a Centaur boy named Bounder. But he was young at the time. He grew to his father's gentleness without losing his own youthful fire. He outlived his human wife and died in my arms, an old man. 'Mellonia,' he said. 'If we meet in the After Life, you will find me that rough young pirate again. The world has aged my body but not my heart. Beware of Elysium unless you're ready to couch with me, and feast on boar meat spitted over an open fire, and drink a toast to every god on high, but especially to my grandmother, Venus, the queen of love.' 'But what about your fa-

ther?' I asked. 'I loved him too. Loved him first.'
'Every other night,' he grinned. 'My father and I
shared everything.' "

"I like Ascanius better."

"I think I loved him better. And what is love to
you?"

He pondered. His young mind seemed to range the
Islands of the Hesperides but, like Theseus' famous
barque, return to port.

"I have seen a cow coupling with a bull. A natural
sight to a shepherd. It doesn't make me ashamed. But
it isn't love. I saw my foster parents sit without touching, without needing to touch, beside a dead fire. That
was love. But not the greatest."

"And the greatest?"

"It can't be explained. It is why men build their
temples. The Iliad is about a war. But a woman
caused the war. When she walked on the walls of
Troy, the battle stopped."

"Yes. Aeneas told me. And how does it come, this
love beyond words?"

"With a rush of wings, I expect."

He could not know that his words were hailstones
bruising a leafless limb.

"Love is a dragonfly. . . ."

"Yes, he is, isn't he? I think I hear him about to
light."

"No. It's only my bees."

"They left a long time ago."

"They must have returned."

"Green-O-the-Woods?"

"Yes?"

"Your bees are gone. The dragonfly may not come. There is only Remus."

It seemed to me that I held an armful of sunflowers against my ancient breasts. No, the flowers were a boy, and the boy had become a god, and I was young in the fashion of princesses. Then I was Danaë to his golden shower. Could I deny the gold?

"Green-O-the-Woods."

"Yes, Fair Hair?"

"Would you like to become a queen?"

I started to say, "But I have already been a queen." Fortunately, Segeta hissed in my ear: "Will you never learn?"

"Yes," I said. "I would like very much to become your queen."

SYLVAN

I

"Sylvan, you're crying!"

"Not! Fauns don't cry. We take things as they come and make light of everything. A bramble scratched my eyes and made them water."

"Both eyes?"

"There were *two* thorns."

"Mellonia may have an herb——"

"No!"

"I realize it was a long wait for you. Sometimes I forgot that a man's time is multiplied by twelve for a Faun."

"I didn't even notice. A fetching Centauress came to pray at the altar. We dallied together among the jonquils."

"Sylvan, you know there aren't any female Centaurs."

"Do you have to be so literal about everything? I was using poetic license."

"Using imagination," he muttered, but he did not press me as we left the circle of oaks.

"The Dryad," I asked. I refused to call her by name. "Was she hospitable?" I wanted to hear him speak of her lightly, a light-o-love, wooed, possessed, and forgotten after a single tryst. (I wanted reassurance that I was not replaced in his heart by an ill-tempered Dryad almost as old as Aeneas.)

"Yes."

"Remus," I chided. "Your spirits seemed mil-dewed. Have you nothing to tell me about her?"

He reminded me suddenly of the aged Faustulus; not weather-beaten, mind you, but sage and delib-erative beyond his years.

"What is there to say about love? It isn't happy, al-together, though it includes happiness. It isn't sad, though it includes sadness. It's a kind of—inter-mingling."

"I should think you would feel like wrestling," I said. "Or drawing one of your goddesses with the lofty breasts. Or swimming the Tiber. You don't look intermingled to me, you look absentminded."

"I am thinking of many things," he said. "Yester-day I wanted to punish the man who killed my mother. I wanted to be a king for the sake of Fauns and runaway slaves and Romulus and my own pride. Now I want to be king for *her* sake, too."

At the mouth of our cave, he stopped and faced me and placed his hands on my shoulders and dissolved me with his searching stare.

"Sylvan, why were you crying back there?"

"I told you once," I snapped. "She must have made you deaf. It's no wonder, an old woman like that."

"Did you think she had driven you out of my heart, little Faun?"

He had not called me "little Faun" since that night

79

a year—twelve years—ago when Romulus stole me from my father's camp.

"Yes," I said, losing control of my tears. "And not to a girl but a witch! Or a squirrel, I should say, the way she lives in a tree and hoards her maidenhead like a choice acorn. Then, gives it away without so much as offering her *other* guest a drink of milk. Remus, she will bite you yet." Because of the goat in me, I sometimes thought of people as animals.

He did not belittle my tears, but touched his fingers, lightly as sunbeams, to dry my cheeks.

"In the circle of oaks," he said, "narcissi and jonquils grow in harmony. There is room for both. Do you understand me, Sylvan?"

"Remus!" Celer, who else? Ass-eyed, he whinnied toward us in a cloud of dust. (Talk about Centaurs! He would have been a donkeysaur if Saturn had thought to include such a beast with the Forest Folk.) The passing year had not improved his eyes or sharpened his thoughts. (If anything, it seemed to have flattened the eyes and dulled the thoughts.)

"Remus," he mumbled as if through a mouth of wine. "News from the city! Romulus wants you in his hut."

In the early dusk, the hut of Romulus was a crouching mist; solemn and dignified, sheep meandered between the huts and, pausing, browsed among sheeplike stones which Vulcan had thrust from his caverns in one of his lesser rages. Shepherds had gathered in silent groups, carefully separated from Romulus' latest recruits, the men from the woods. The new men wore the familiar loin cloth, the thong sandals, of rustics in every trade, but the weapons they carried were daggers, not staves, and their faces, though mostly young, were scarred and sullen; their eyes stared rapine and theft. One, I knew, had fled from Lavinium after killing his wife; another had robbed a temple and murdered a priest in Cumae, a new Greek colony rising to the south. Remus disliked them; Romulus gave them huts and welcomed their knives but did not trust them. Celer drank with them.

The wife-killer saw me and jabbed a mate in the ribs. "What kind of army is this? Hooves instead of sandals?" He puffed his cheeks and baaed like a goat.

"Sylvan," said Remus, angry as bees, a whole hive of them, with a pilfering bear. "Leave him to me. I know how to treat such a lout."

"It's only a jest," I said, shoving him out of danger with my hoof. Then, to my heckler: "You sound like a frog. Do it like this." I bleated until the she-goats answered in every pen. "Want to try again?" He busied himself with cleaning his knife. Mockery silenced him better than blows.

A figure loomed at us out of the mist, a tall ship scudding through overcast seas. It was Romulus. To me he nodded; his condescension reduced me to a goat. He envied, I think, the time which I spent with his brother. To Remus he smiled; predator become protector.

"Brother," he said. "Balbus is here from the city. He has brought us news."

In the circular hut, surrounded by eager listeners, the dormouse had roused from his dream. He welcomed us as a new audience.

"Remus," he said, flicking an errant whisker. "And Sylvan, is it not? Listen to what I have seen. I saw Numitor in the market yesterday with his chamberlain. Lately Amulius has allowed him considerable freedom. To appease the people, no doubt, and keep them from growling about the latest tax on swine. Besides, Numitor is much too old to be a threat. His eyes are dim from watching the stars, and he has to walk with a staff. Anyway, a half-grown sheep dog ran at one of Amulius' soldiers. Friendly. Wanting to play. But the soldier didn't. He raised his spear and impaled the dog on its point and flung the carcass into a drainage ditch. 'Coward,' cried Numitor. Stooped, nearsighted, he had still seen more than he liked. He raised his staff to strike the man. The soldier, far from cowed, wiped the blood from his spear —one of those cruel barbed spears which enter cleanly but tear the flesh when you draw them out— and faced the former king with an arrogant smile. 'Old man,' he said, 'there's room in the ditch for *you*.' Numitor's chamberlain hurried him back to the palace.

"As we left the market, he waved his staff and shouted, 'If my grandsons had lived, there would be no soldiers in town!' The onlookers broke into a cheer and hissed the soldiers, and someone close to me, though I never saw his face, said to a friend, 'There is talk in the country of twins who would be just the age —' I did not hear the rest. I thought to myself: Romulus will know."

Romulus shrugged. "I know of no twins on the Palatine. Perhaps the Quirinal, among the Sabines— But sons of Mars! A pretty dream at best. At any rate, we are kingless here. Do you wonder we stay in the country?"

Sleepily Balbus scrutinized the twins, the bellower and the persuader; the stalwart and the slim; the dark and the fair. Still, there were likenesses: the stubborn set of the mouths, the tilt of the chins, the level, fearless eyes. In a word, regality if not divinity. Sometimes the shepherds called them Castor and Pollus. Sleepy Balbus perhaps had surmised the truth.

"When I think of Amulius," he said, "I am tempted to stay here with you on the Palatine. They call him the Owl in town, you know, though he calls himself the Lion. But Marcus, my master, depends on me to bring him news of his herds. Thirty newborn lambs, you say. The wolves keep to the forest. Thieves are a nuisance but not a threat. Good work, Romulus. You too, Remus. And you, Sylvan—I expect you have a special way with the beasts. Goats anyway. Goodbye, goodbye, I'm off to the town."

Whiskers puffed in the breeze, lurching from side to side, he bobbled down the hill.

"Goats indeed! The man needs a tail himself."

"Like yours, Sylvan?"

"Something more functional. Balance, don't you see. There's an animal the Telesphori remember from the east." The hooded healers were not indigenous to the forest. Anticipating the Etruscans, they had migrated from an unidentified land which they called the Rising Sun. "The southeast, to be exact. As you know, they've been everywhere and seen everything. I believe it's called a kangagrew. It has a tail like a battering ram which it uses for balance and propulsion, or a seat when it's tired."

"Sylvan!"

"I'm not exaggerating at *all*. What is more, it keeps a garden of eucalyptus trees, and it has a basket in its stomach for carrying a dinner of leaves and twigs when it goes on a trip. Hence, the name— kanga-*grew*."

In Romulus' hut, Faustulus, Celer, the twins, and I remained by the fire to evaluate the news, Remus always included me in his councils.

Romulus looked like his second name. I have called his face both handsome and cruel. Now, I did not think of adjectives. The name implied the nature: Wolf.

"We have waited with patience," he said. "At last the mood of the city appears to be right. They will flock to our side as soon as they know us for princes!

But first they have to be told. Numitor"—it was Remus who always said 'Grandfather'—"is the one to tell them. First we must introduce ourselves to him. I will go to Alba Longa tomorrow and seek an audience."

"But he lives in Amulius' palace," objected Faustulus, bent as a hickory bow but taut, like Romulus, with the rage to revolt. "How can you get an audience?"

"He's right," said Remus. "You can't simply walk up to the palace and ask to see Grandfather. Alba Longa is not Veii. Amulius' guards are much too suspicious. Your height and bearing set you apart at once. You *look* like the son of a god. I should be the one to go."

"And what do you look like, Remus? A rustic? Blind men in Latium are as rare as virgins in Etruria. They will take you for a spy from the Gauls. Even if they don't, how will you gain an audience with Numitor?"

"First I will change the color of my hair. You've seen the umber along the banks of the Tiber? Women use it for dye, I am told. Robes, rugs, coverlets—I will dye my hair and dirty my face into a low, thievish countenance."

"Impossible."

"What's that, Sylvan?"

"Can't."

"Pass for a thief? I'll put a squint in my eye and a sidelong lurch in my step. Not even you will know me for your friend." He cocked his eye and lowered his shoulder and shuffled around the hut with assorted, and so he thought, alarming snorts. He was not remotely thievish, he was Remus playing at thief. But who was I to spoil his fun? "Then I will steal one of Grandfather's cows. His shepherds will catch me and take me to receive his justice. In the theft of cows, the owner and not the king has the right to pass judgment. Amulius will have no hand in this unless my own grandfather turns me over to him. I don't believe he will."

"No," said Romulus. "It is much too dangerous. I won't let you take the risk."

Usually I wanted to kick him with both of my hooves. Now I wanted to hug him.

"Remus is right," said that asinine Celer, mouthing his usual monosyllables. "Old men love him. He's soft and polite and he drinks like a girl. Let him go, Romulus. I have a stake in this too."

Yes, I thought, riches to spend and a house in which to wench. What do you know of laws and government and justice for Fauns as well as men?

"It's settled then," said Remus.

"No!" I bleated.

"Sylvan, what is it now?"

"You can only go if you take me along to look after you."

"Certainly not. I'm older than you."

"Not any more. I had a birthday yesterday. Nineteen." (Nineteen and still a virgin! Venus, where have you been?)

"Months, not years."

"It's the same thing for me."

"Sorry, Sylvan, it's out of the question. Fauns are rare in Latium. How could we hide your ears? The soldiers might catch you and put you into a show."

Romulus frowned and stroked his beginning beard. This fierce, ambitious young man, who feared neither wolves nor warriors, was unashamedly fearful for his brother's life. At last, like a father sending his son to fight the Gauls, he placed his hands on Remus' shoulders.

"Go with my blessings, Brother. Meanwhile, I'll gather our shepherds."

"And thieves," I added.

"And await your return. If you don't return in a day—"

"Give me two."

"Two days then and we'll come to get you. The gate may be bronze, but the walls aren't high to shepherds who live on hills."

"Or to shepherds led by princes." Faustulus opened his mighty arms and embraced the twins. Faustulus, bent but still the Oak. Even Romulus dwindled in his shade. "For eighteen years I have called you my sons. Now, like the she-wolf who brought you to my door, I must step aside and return you to your royal kin. You will not shame him."

87

II

The next morning, Remus knelt and veiled his head in a cloak and prayed to his special god. Years of wearing had not effaced the meticulous carven features: the full, boyish cheeks, the hand outstretching barley like a wand.

"Vaticanus, god of beginnings, begin my journey with luck: See me to Alba Longa and I will take it from there."

After the prayer, he carved a niche in the clay above the couch, enshrined the god, and placed an acorn of milk before his feet. Every one knows that the gods, whether men and women or bodiless powers in the wind, the rock, the tree, encourage and relish offerings of food. The acorn, a parting gift from the Squirrel, was hollow, its round miniscule walls were glazed with hardened wax, its bottom was flat like that of a cup. Wall niches . . . acorn cups . . . Mellonia had invaded our cave. I dreaded the day when she came to live with us; worse, invited us to her tree; worse, invited Remus and Luperca but excluded me.

Luperca, no respecter of divinity, eyed the milk. She could climb the couch—in Remus' absence, she often *slept* on the couch—and reach the niche with her tongue. A single lap would envelop the cup as

well as its contents. I did not begrudge the god his offering, but Mellonia's cup was definitely expendable.
Perhaps a slight nudge. . . .

"Now for my bees," said Remus. "Look after them,
will you? And Luperca too. You may have to coax
her to eat. She is very feeble." (Ha!) "And Sylvan.
Will you tell Mellonia where I have gone? I had promised to visit her today."

I stamped my hoof. "The Squirrel Lady?"

"Demi-goddess."

"Demi-goddess? She can't outlive her tree!"

"But her tree has lived for a thousand years, and
will live a thousand more. Till Saturn returns. Then
he will find her another."

"Is that what she told you? What about lightning?
Floods? Woodcutters? Mangy, smelly, lecherous
Fauns?"

"Your ears are quivering," he grinned. "They always do when you're angry." He stroked them with
his irresistible fingers. "You will see Mellonia?
Promise me, Sylvan."

"Don't do that," I cried. "You know how it
tickles."

"But you like to be tickled."

"That's my point. You can make me promise anything."

"Would you rather I yanked your tail?"

"All right, all right. I will see Mellonia. Now go
and steal your cow."

Can you doubt that I followed him? It was part of my plan. Once we reached the herd, I proposed to blend with a sere, brownish bush until he began his theft—then, like a crafty accomplice, rush to his side and share his guilt. I was careful to keep a tree or a hill between us. In places where Remus left no sandal tracks, I kept to the trail with the help of my keen ears. In the marshy ground, I did not squish my hooves among the sedges, and even the Sabine burial mounds, some of them freshly heaped and haunted, no doubt, by disgruntled spirits reluctant to lose the sun, could not alarm me into a giveaway gallop.

Numitor's shepherds drowsed in the shade of a hayrick, men as old as their master because, it was said, he only hired the aged; the young reminded him of his daughter and grandsons. A one-eyed sheep dog took his ease at their feet. If the state of his eyesight indicated the shape of his teeth, he posed no threat to my tail. I chose a blackberry copse for my hideaway and waited for Remus to begin his theft.

The wait was short, even for a Faun. From a herd which lacked the energy to ruminate, much less graze, Remus selected a thin, particularly listless cow whose udder resembled a hive deserted by bees. The dog blinked his eye as the three shepherds continued to drowse.

"Shoo, cow, off with you!" Remus cried, trampling the bushes to compensate for the cow's inaction (perhaps she had died on her feet).

The dog gave a hypocritical flick of his tail when

he saw his masters open their eyes (the Fauns have a saying: 'The tail tells the tale'.).

"There's a thief in the herd," said one of the men as he might have said, "Pass the cheese."

"Yes," sighed the leader, the youngest of the three, a spry seventy-five I judged. "I expect we'll have to teach him a lesson. Cyclops, sic him." He shoved the dog in the rump. Cyclops began to cough; charitably, I should say that he began to bark.

Remus pretended to be bewildered by the barks. He cast about him for an avenue of escape. *Here, the intransigent cow; there, the rapacious dog and three vigilant shepherds armed with staffs.* He threw up his hands as if to ward off horns or blows and confess defeat. It was time to enter the fray. I stomped my hooves, bleated, and thundered into the field.

"Sylvan," he cried, "I told you not to come!" But his grin was an invitation. Our second Adventure. (The first I preferred to forget.)

"Two of them," croaked the leader. "And one with horns! Devilish work afoot."

Cautiously they approached the beleaguered cow, who, however, continued her inactivities (no, she had not died on her feet. The flies alit but did not lodge). The dog, meanwhile, preening himself on his vigilance, barked wispily at their heels.

"Brave dog, brave Cyclops," the leader said, stroking the beast on its flea-bitten head. One of his friends fetched leathern thongs, designed for binding the legs of calves, from a lean-to beside the hayrick.

"Now then. Bind their hands."

Glowering though not struggling, we offered our hands to the thongs. Among the three of them, they managed to bind us, to prod us with their staffs, and to quiet Cyclops before he exhausted his breath and lost his cough.

"They are just boys," said the oldest man—if Faustulus was an oak, this man was an elm who had undergone a pestilence. "Need we take them to Numitor in town? It's such a long walk, Julius. A good thrashing may be all they need."

Remus hurried to speak. I will have to say that he tried his best to hulk menacingly and snarl. "My father thrashed me once with a hickory cane."

"Eh? Speak up, boy."

"That's why I ran away and became a thief. No, you will have to take us to Numitor, unless you want your cows—bulls too—stolen and sold to the Etruscans across the river." He tilted his head to a rakish angle. "And my friend here, the Faun. Would you believe it? Young as he is, he's already carried off six virgins." He added proudly, "I've carried off seven. But then I started sooner."

"I learn fast," I leered. "Eh, Cutthroat?"

"Boys they may be," sighed the leader, "but renegades, and dangerous. Numitor will have to judge. Can the two of you get them to town while Cyclops and I watch the herds?"

The old men looked at each other and then toward Alba Longa, weighing no doubt the hazardous

half day's walk with renegades. One of them prod-
ded me with his staff.

"Watch that tail," I snapped.

"Lurch," hissed Remus.

I gave a belated lurch.

"We'll do our best," sighed the prodder. "The one
with horns—is he called a Centaur?"

"Centaurs are *horse*-men, imbecile. Do horses
have horns? Do horses have quaint, decorative tails
which look like silk? Do—?"

I felt Remus' nudge.

"That's right. A Centaur. You can tell by the hairy
flanks and the smell."

"That's your own flea-bitten dog!"

"Give him a whack if he starts to talk dirty," advised the leader. "Ho there, blackguards! Off to the
town with you."

Alba Longa, the 'city' of Remus' dream, was in
truth a modest town whose only fortifications were
its walls and its gate. The crenellated walls, though
high, had been cracked by Vulcan, the Earthquaker,
and pitted by Jove, the Thunderer. The bronze gate,
though thick, had been blackened by many weathers.
The streets intermingled grass with cobblestones and
dwindled into tenuous lanes. Nevertheless, the town
was a Troy compared to the Palatine. The larger
houses were smooth and white with plaster and
looked to country boys like little palaces.

"And their roofs," Remus gasped. "They are cov-

ered with baked clay shingles." We were used to the
thatches of shepherd huts. "No danger of fire, no rain
soaking through."

"Ho there!" shouted our more vociferous captor,
the Elm.

"Rapscallions!" shouted his friend, and people
paused in their conversation, stopped their work,
peered from doors to watch the advance of a rene-
gade Faun and his human cohort. Five thousand people inhabited the town, not including the goats, and
most of them seemed to be in the streets to greet
our arrival (including the goats).

"Stole six virgins, the Centaur did."

"Friend stole *seven*."

Then, the marketplace. . . .

Colored canvass stalls for the merchants and the
farmers, and altars for the gods who deserved less
than temples but more than neglect. . . . Red and
black and yellow and purple morning glories unfold-
ing to the day. . . . Between them, marble stones
like white periwinkles: Sylvanus, Vulcan, Faunus,
Picus, Volumnus. . . .

"And who is *he?*" I asked, pointing to an altar so
small that a large-bottomed fishwife, fanning herself
with a sponge, was enveloping everything except the
name of the god.

"Must be Minutius, the god of trifles. Balbus says
you worship him for luck in little everyday transac-
tions, like getting a good price for your fish."

"Stop that back talk."

"I wonder if Minutius can blight a pestilential elm."

A Vestal, carrying water atop her head in a black Etruscan vase, glimpsed my flanks, dropped the vessel, and shattered the porous clay. A vintner spilled a pigskin and a moist tracery spiderwebbed the stones. A barber poised a razor above an olive-oiled throat, a Damocles sword in miniature. Farmers mistakenly traded melons for wilted lettuces and lost their cabbages to enterprising goats. Children and sheep dogs scrambled to give us room in the streets.

Not, however, the hired mercenaries of Amulius, brash and ubiquitous in every square. Latin cities in general raised an army only to fight a war. But Amulius needed his army to keep him in power. What he could not raise he rented from Sparta, Carthage, and Veii: men who sold their strength as a whore sells her charms; measured for backs and biceps as she for breasts and buttocks.

"Remus," I whispered. "That woman with gold bangles and restless bosom. See her giving us the eye? What do you think she does for a livelihood?"

"Plies."

"My thoughts exactly. After we meet your grandfather, do you think we might—I might—get plied?"

"Business first."

"It's all very well for you to talk. You have the Squirrel. Im a middle-aged virgin."

"What about the Centauress?"

"Ho there," shouted our captors—I could not commend the variety of their exhortation—until a soldier swatted them on their heads with the shaft of his spear.

"Hush, old men. You're near the palace." Proddings ceased together with castigations, but not the stares of the crowd.

The circular temple of Vesta, raised by Etruscan architects on a stone platform, twinkled with terra cotta tiles, orange in the afternoon sun, and opposite the temple crouched the palace of Amulius, a low white rectangle distinguished only by size from the better houses. Amulius hoped, we had heard, to build an Etruscan palace, multi-colored instead of white, with frescoes and collonnades and images of his patron deity, Jupiter; the taxes he stole, the cattle, the wine, the wool, he would trade to the king of Veii for architects and sculptors.

As a start, at least, he had flanked his gate with bronze Etruscan lions, slender of flank and lithe of limb, their tails looped gracefully over their backs to touch their manes; their eyes like those of their sculptors, slanted and strange, cruel in the shadows, kind in the sun.

The guardian lions in turn were guarded by two Etruscan warriors who looked Olympian thoughts and dreamed, no doubt, of many-templed Veii, the city of a thousand images, and bronze Tarquinia, the city named for a king.

"Have you business in the King's palace?" one of them deigned to ask. He did not berate us like the soldiers in the street. A god, he did not need to be-rate; rather, he condescended. It lay in his power to judge, reject, or admit. His jerkin was tanned leather, his crested helmet, bronze. (He smelled, however, of sweat. Most men are slightly rancid to a Faun's sharp nose. Not Remus. He always smelled of the woods.)

Our captors, being shepherds, were ill at ease in town. The soldiers had scared them, the guards awed them to stammering incoherence. Remus had to ex-plain our presence.

"They caught us stealing Numitor's cattle. We want to receive his judgment."

"Numitor, you say?" Condescension became con-cern. He climbed the stairs between the flanking lions —devoured, so it seemed, only to be disgorged with a brisk little man who skipped down the stairs like an amorous water bug. Numitor's Chamberlain. Twit-tering thanks to the shepherds, dismissing the guard, he ushered us through a hallway supported by wooden timbers and into a walled garden behind the palace. Roses rioted up the wall in vermillion succu-lence and crocuses dipped like golden goblets beside a lotus pool. I wanted to roll in the flowers and kick my hooves in the air.

Numitor sat in a backless chair and stared inscrut-ably into the pool. His white curving hair was hardly distinguishable from his white robes, which billowed around his feet and hid his sandals. He made me think of a cloud about to return to the sky.

The Chamberlain had to announce our presence.

"Prince, your faithful shepherds have brought two thieves to receive your justice."

Sighing, he raised his head and looked at us without expression. His face was as yellow and cracked as papyrus, laid in a tomb by pharaohs as old as the Pyramids; god-men ruling the Nile before the Etruscans had passed through Egypt and brought her lore to Italy. A face like papyrus whose writing had been erased by time; a palimpsest, awaiting new inscriptions.

"Bring them forward," he said.

Remus fell to his knees and kissed Numitor's feet. He seemed to have lost his tongue in the stress of the moment (or the awkwardness of his position?). I wanted to lend him a Faun's facility.

He did not need my help.

"*My king.*" Love, reverence, obedience reverberated in the simple words.

Numitor withdrew his hand and wearily motioned the boy to rise. "I am not your king," he sighed. "I never was. You are much too young—the age of my grandsons, had they lived. And they were born when I had lost my throne. Tell me, boy, why did you steal my cattle? In spite of your dirt, you don't look like a thief."

"Because I wanted to see you."

"To see me? I don't understand."

"As a thief, I knew they would bring me to receive your judgment."

"You were right. Before I deliver judgment, what favour do you ask? I warn you, I have few to give."

"Your blessing. Your love."

"An old man loves his children. I have none. His grandchildren. I have none. My heart is a nest without any swallows. It has forgotten love. But tell me your name. Something about you stirs me—"

"A shepherd named me Remus, and my brother, Romulus. We are twins."

The names, of course, were meaningless to him, but he caught at the last word. "Twins, you say?"

"A month after we were born, our mother was buried alive in a pit and we were sent to be drowned in the Tiber. But Faustulus, the shepherd, saved us and made us his sons."

The papyrus revealed its cracks as loss, anger, anguish; the griefs of a dreamer defeated by the truth (or an actor defeated by his role?); the palimpsest had recovered its characters.

A groan welled from his lips, like a shudder from one of those deep-dug borax shafts of Vulcan, which, silent for years, erupt with hisses and thunder.

"What are you saying? Why do you torture an old man with your heartless lies? I saw my grandson when Amulius took them from my daughter. One was dark. Darker than you. One was gold, gold like this flower." He crushed a crocus majestically under his sandal. "A gift from the god, his father. Which are you?" The speech was genuine, I had no doubt.

Still, there was something calculated about the gestures and the pauses. Exiled Sovereign. Bereaved Parent. He postured even as he suffered. He was one of those men who, unknown even to themselves, belong in an Etruscan circus.

"The gold." Remus fell to his knees and ducked his head in the pool; he scraped and worried the umber from his flaxen locks. He had knelt a shepherd; he rose a prince, crowned with his own gold.

"Here boy, let me feel what I cannot yet believe. Soft as a baby's hair. Hers was soft like that. But not gold. That was from Mars. Hair like woven sunlight. A god's hair. Speak to me again. Call me—"

"Grandfather."

"Enough, enough."

He clasped the boy to his breast. "Rhea," he sobbed, "your son has come home to me."

"You are a senile old fool!"

I knew the man I had never met and not by his robe; I knew him by his hunched and dwarfish shape, the eyes which were crafty instead of wise. The Owl.

"Go to Romulus," Remus whispered. "I will try to hold them off."

Behind me a prince and a tyrant grappled among the roses. With a single kick of my hooves, I vaulted the garden walls.

"Vaticanus," I prayed, "help me to bring him help! Yes, even from *her*."

I landed on hooves and hands behind the palace. The cobblestones gave me a jolt and took my wind. Momentarily, I must have resembled a goat. A crumpled old woman, carrying melons like vicarious breasts, paused in mild surprise.

"Young man, are you a goat or a Faun?"

Erect, I glared her an answer.

"A Faun then. . . . Never saw one before. Heard about them though. Oh well, I'm too old to rape. That's Venus for you. Gives you the wherewithal. First thing you know its wherewithout." She turned her back with a shrug which seemed to say: "Thieving Fauns are Amulius' business. Steal him blind for all I care."

The street, cramped, rank with refuse, parching in the sun, could not even boast a soldier or a guard. A solitary ass, tethered to a stake, watched me vacantly through his flat, Celer-like eyes. Perhaps his master had business in the shop of the fabric dyer, its sign a bronze trumpet shell, the source of dye for aristocrats who wished to ape the royal purple of the murex.

Remus had given me an inch of time. The guards who had answered Amulius' call would surely come for me. I must reach the gate; in short, I must race like Remus. But a running Faun in a city of men and women ruled by a tyrant would look like a thief or a runaway from a show.

"Ass," I said, "you're going to help me, like it or not." He gave me a vacuous stare. I loosed his rope, and thinking of Celer, hoofed him in the rump. He was obviously indolent and he pretended to be ignorant, but he knew how to run.

"Whoa, whoa," I shouted, galloping after him to recover escaping property. A Faun pursuing an ass? Remarkable. Laughable. Believable. We attracted stares from soldiers, smiles from children, commiseration from goats. Still, we made a convincing pair. I did not skulk; I did not look like a thief; and *he* was the runaway.

Ahead of us loomed the gate, open for farmers and shepherds; the twin towers bristling like a pair of griffins with archer slits and battlements. Ahead of us stared Amulius' guards. One of them snatched solicitously at the donkey's tail; but sweaty tails, even if tufted, elude the firmest grip.

"Let him go," he advised. "Hunger 'ull fetch him back."

"Can't. Wolves might get him."

Free of the gate, free of the onlookers, the wellwishers, the guards we encountered a potter bringing his pots to town in a stone-wheeled cart. Mouthing imprecations, he spun his cart to escape our headlong flight and spilled his load. Lamps of terra cotta, dyed and glazed to a high finish, tumbled and broke into a heap of shards.

"Laverna crack your skull," he cried. The goddess of thieves was not a friend to the honest. She trafficked in curses, imprecations, and accidents. Well, I had told enough lies in my time to win immunity; in fact, she probably considered me one of her priests.

"Friend of mine," I called after me. "Try Faunus."

To the left of the road and below the town, Lake Albanus epitomized the sea, and skiffs of alder poised like dragonflies on her lapis lazuli. Ahead of me wound the basalt road to Veii, patrolled by soldiers and driven by two-wheeled chariots and horses with tails which, thanks to the glue extracted from the hooves of goats, stood as stiff and perpendicular as masts, their plumes abillow with wind.

"Here we must separate," I said to the ass, grateful for services however unwillingly offered, and I chose a path among dusky cypresses.

Romulus, tending sheep with a careful eye to the woods, saw me before I had climbed the Palatine; overtook me before I could reach the top.

"Sylvan!" No longer was I the Goat; I was his brother's friend.

I told him about the scene in the palace garden; Remus' capture; my escape. Swearing, he drove his staff in the ground.

"I knew I should have gone."

"Who can say no to Remus?"

"He let *you* go."

"Not at first. I had to follow and lurk."

"I'll burn the last bloody building. Yes, the temple to Vesta too. What did she ever do to help my mother? See if I don't. Celer, watch the cattle." He hurried me into his hut to confer with Faustulus. I might have been one of his trusted generals.

"Sylvan, tell your story."

I repeated the facts without embellishments, no mean task for a Faun.

"Faustulus, we attack tomorrow night!"

"But the people won't even recognize us," the Oak objected. "Remus was captured before he could tell Numitor about our plans. Right, Sylvan?"

I tried to puff myself into a general. "Right!"

"No matter. We can't delay. Once in the city, we'll shout in unison—'Long live Numitor!'—and rally support."

Faustulus shook his head. "You know I love the boy. But what can we do against walls and mercenaries? I would suggest a form of ransom."

"And show our strength? Amulius takes us for motley shepherds, not a gathering army. We'll use an oak for a battering ram."

"Against bronze?"

"Well, then. Scale the walls."

"Where are your ladders? Where are our scaffolds?"

"Ladders are easy to build. Take them by surprise and——"

"Alba Longa stands on a hill. You come within range of their archers once you leave the woods."

"Then too," I interjected, "what will they do to Remus once they see us coming?"

"They'll be too busy to think about him. At any rate, we'll head straight for the palace to set him free. . . ."

Boasts, arguments, objections. . . .

Escaping the hut, I fled toward the twining path to Remus' cave. I wanted to think and plan, not bluster and vaunt. I wanted to rescue Remus more than to topple a King. (Give Romulus his due, so did he.) Unfortunately, I met an obstacle across my path. Celer with Romulus' sheep; Celer, excluded for once from the council of war; not contentious, it seemed, but languid and mocking. He lolled in the shade of a rock, staff beside him, a straw between his teeth. If a wolf had stolen his flock, I do not think that he would have left his shade.

"So they shut the Woodpecker in a cage," he smirked. "Big Games tomorrow, eh?" Before I could hoof him, he changed the subject. "Sylvan, I hear you found a Dryad."

"Who told you?"

"Remus told Romulus. He wants her to be his queen."

"And Romulus told you." Well, even ill-tempered squirrels did not deserve Celer.

"We could share her," he said, "if you show me her tree. We'll do her a favor. You know what Dryads like."

"Look for her north of the Palatine," I lied. "An ilex tree with a lightning mark on the trunk."

"I think I saw a Dryad once," he said. "Oh, sixteen or seventeen years ago. Mistook her for a shepherd's girl at the time. Looked for her later when I left Amulius' service and came to the Palatine."

105

(Amulius had fired him, in fact: assaulting a woman in the streets.) "Looked on the hills too. No such girl. Milky skin. Green, slanted eyes. Do you know, at the time I thought I saw her pointed ears. No, I told myself. A trick of the light. Do you think it could be the same?"

"Possibly," I said. "This one is old and hideous. She looks like a fig sucked dry by wasps. Seventeen years can make a difference, *you* should know."

I lowered my ears and fled to my cave. My view of Mellonia was undergoing a change. If she had contended with men like Celer, four hundred and eighty-seven years of them, perhaps she should be forgiven her temper and petulance.

Luperca pressed her nose against my leg. It was time for a truce. She sensed her master's plight.

I knelt and took her head between my hands.

"Luperca," I said. "Remus has gone to the city. They have taken him captive. He told me to tell the Squirrel. But what can she do?" Remus could talk to her. He claimed to understand her looks and growls. I shook my head in despair.

Then I remembered the bees. Even in the cave, I could hear their loud and prosperous nest. Mellonia had miraculously saved the hive. Might she not know miracles to use in war? She had loved two kings. She had been a queen.

I replenished Luperca's bowl with curds and milk. She had not molested the offering in the niche of the god.

"Wait here," I said. "I am going to find a queen."

At last I could read her eyes: "My mistress?"

"Yes."

She followed me from the cave with the air of one who knows her destination. I lost her among the trees.

Above me a conch shell boomed from the Palatine:

Romulus calling his men to probable rout; to Remus' ruin.

MELLONIA

I

"Niece, why are you twisting your hair? There are easier ways of making yarn."

"I am going to weave a tapestry. Penelope, don't you see. I need her patience."

"He'll come, believe me, my dear."

"How do you know what a boy will do?"

"Look in your mirror. Even with twisted hair, you can hardly pass for a Gorgon. Calypso, Circe, Helen —*not* Medusa."

"Boys break promises."

"Mellonia." She only used my name before a severe reprimand. "I think I should call you Cassandra. Prophesying doom as most young women—yes, young—predict weddings. And Aeneas took one look at you and forgot Dido."

"Aunt," I cried. "I don't want to tempt the gods. Juno, who hated Aeneas. Venus—I may have affronted her with my chastity. I love him too much, you see. He will be the death of me."

"Or the life?" she chuckled. Purple grew amethystine; her sudden shimmering was a smile; I knew what she had in mind (in mist?).

Then, the knock at the foot of the tree. The kick of a hoof.

Sylvan.

"Come through the tunnel," I called from the window above his head. "You know the way." To Segeta: "Go now. At once. Fauns are afraid of Lemures."

"Oh, very well. But I wanted to see his horns. You know, I have always fancied Fauns. My first six lovers——"

"Please!"

"If Remus doesn't come . . . now that you've broken your fast, I mean. He seems a presentable chap. Experienced too, I expect."

"No more lentils and beans. Ever!"

"I have brought you news." Hesitant, he stood at the top of the stairs. He had combed his hair and caught it behind his head with a tendril of wild grapevine; sleek, silken, brown as a chestnut. He had even girded his flanks in a loin cloth. He had dressed to call.

I drew him into the room. Remus' friend. My friend too if I could learn to deserve him. I wanted to hold him, childlike, in my arms. The thought of his brown head, warm against my breast, warmed me like a brazier in the frost. To hold, to cradle, simply to touch, a mother with her child—lost sensations, remembered but not without pain. So much to re-learn. . . . Still, there was time. There must be time.

"He is going to follow you here?"

"He went to the palace to see his grandfather, Numitor. Amulius surprised him in the garden. Called his guards."

I felt the familiar rat at my heart. "Is he hurt?"

"Not when I left."

"And Romulus—what will he do?"

He explained the plans he had overheard in the hut.

"Romulus' shepherds," I muttered. "I have seen them drill in the woods. Boys and cutthroats. They have no armor, weapons, catapults."

"They are making shields out of animal hides."

"Hides against archers?"

"I think they are making ladders to climb the walls."

"What is a staff against a sword?"

"Green-O-the-Woods," he said. I liked the name from his lips. Fauns have a lilt in their voices; he semed to sing the name. "You have hurt a bee."

"What? Oh, poor little worker. I must have shaken my hands and flung her onto the floor." I lent my finger to her small hooked feet and set her among my asphodels.

"Remus would like what you did."

"And Romulus?"

"He would have crushed the bee between his fingers."

"It was so when he was a child. He frightened me even then."

"Mellonia," he cried, seizing my hand, dropping it rather as if he had seized a holy relic.

"Here," I said, pressing his stubby fingers. "Tell me your heart." It is rare that a friend can say: "At one precise moment I began to love you." The love which is friendship grows like a poplar tree, a ring at a time; roots, trunk, branches, leaves. But time was compressed for me as well as Sylvan. I loved him for loving Remus: The poplar lacked no leaf.

"Mellonia, you can save him. Not Romulus. Only you. You are a queen!"

"Dearest Sylvan. Where are my subjects? I have given myself too long to winter."

"Queenliness lies in the heart."

"My heart was a mausoleum. Remus opened the door. Still, there is dust."

"Dust can be swept away."

"Have you the broom?"

"No," he said. "It is for you to clean. And now."

I touched his cheek with my fingertips. Smooth, beardless cheek. Boy's cheek. "I will try to remember the ways of a queen." Cassandra prophesied doom. Penelope dared to hope.

"Such things are never lost. I could as soon forget how to butt."

"You are a rare friend to him, Sylvan. You and I, we are his friends. Perhaps we can save him. Return to Romulus. Tell him to gather his men below the city. Tomorrow night. Hidden but watchful. Watch Arcturus. When the temple of Vesta catches the light of the star, I will come to him in the woods."

"Alone?"

"If I come alone, he is lost. But the forest was once my friend."

"Once?"

"I have lived to myself and fed on bitterness. I am like a tree whose roots have drunk the brine of sea caves and withered the parent trunk."

"You sheltered a woodpecker and a flea-bitten wolf. If that isn't friendship——"

"But not the rest. I sheltered the few who came in search. I did not go to the many. Now, even Luperca seems to have forsaken me. She is not in your cave?"

"No. I thought she had come to you."

"I must visit the King."

"What king is this, Mellonia? Fauns have no kings, nor bears, nor wolves. Only men, so I thought."

"The King without a crown."

"The Valley of the Blue Monkeys! The home of the Telesphori. But no one can enter the place. You know that. They will come to you in their green hoods and smile and bow and turn you away with a gift."

I pressed his hand, smooth, stubby, that of a child. "I will not accept the gift."

"Mellonia, I haven't been kind to you."

"Sylvan, it was I who was cruel. I reviled you at the first. Called you an Acorn-Eater. You have done nothing except befriend my friend."

"I was jealous of you. I called you worse than Acorn-Eater behind your back. The Squirrel Lady!"

"For most of my life—since Aeneas died—I have hated Fauns on sight. Thought them lechers and liars."

"Sometimes we are."

"Not you, Sylvan. Never you. A man is the sum of his friends. Remus loves you more than Romulus. More, I think, than me. I have built him a child's tree house with grapevines and hempen ladders. I have built with dreams. You have built him a woodman's house of mortar and beams. Solidly, and for the years. You have built with truth. I am his lover. You are his friend. Let us join together, piling truth upon dream, strength upon strength, as Neptune piled his stones to build the walls of Troy. The sum of our friendship shall make him a king."

He set his hoof to the stair to leave my room, my house, my tenuous hope. The gesture was oddly touching. The animal part of him might have been Luperca; the boy-part, Cuckoo.

"Sylvan, wait. In truth I am afraid for him. The forest is restless. The cranes have been flying in aimless circles, trailing their legs like anchors, as they do before a storm. All last night, the owls hooted and fluttered among my limbs and did not let me sleep. I have looked in vain for vultures, birds of good omen."

"Good omens? You are Remus' good omen."

I went in search of the King.

II

The Valley was not of the forest; it hid within the forest, like Hope in Pandora's Box. It did not stand on a hill; it cupped into a valley which seemed a hollowed hill, overturned; smoothly rounded in spite of its flourishing; deep but not mountain-deep. To some the place must have seemed a door to the Underworld; I would have said to Elysium.

Oak and ilex did not encroach in the door, nor rowan, hickory, and elm. Underground springs, some of them chill from the mountains, some of them hot with the breath of Vulcan, scattered a rootlike network under the valley, erupting at times into geysers, warming a bamboo grove, cooling a glade among mahogany trees; at any time of the day, at any season, you could exult with spring, nest in autumn. Storms swept over the place but could not find the door. Snowflakes melted before they struck the ground. Drouths sered the trees around the rim, but the greenery knew no blight in the Valley of the Blue Monkeys.

I stood at the top of a path of round green stones, malachites the size of lily pads—I, a sometime queen —and waited humbly for welcome or rejection. I did not speak; I did not need to speak. I had bared my breasts like a lady of sea-girt Crete, those emblems less of desire than motherhood. I wore a flaring skirt in the shape of a saffron crocus; my necklace, an onyx dolphin with amber eyes; my slippers, antelope leather with clasps of ivory. My hair, unfilleted, fell to my shoulders like a rain of leaves. My crown was a murex shell of beaten gold, inlaid with starfish of lapis lazuli. Thus had I dressed when Ascanius called me his queen—"Queen of the forest, dressed for the King of the sea. . . ."

The gown had lain in a cedar chest, age upon useless age, together with my heart.

I watched the trees, hushed of wind and bird. . . . Then, a faint, faraway chatter as musical as song. . . . Hidden at first, the singers. . . . Glimpsed at last like will-o-the-wisp. . . . Blue fires flickering in a green dusk. . . . Blue monkeys.

At the same time, I saw the messenger climbing the path, the familiar green hood, the pink, boyish features of Lordon, the shyest of those three Telesphori who had carried gifts to the twins; the sweet singer.

"Mellonia," he cried, wanting I think to seize my hand. "Have you come to see our King?" He stood a little in awe of me; I had not seen him since he had brought his gift to the twins. He came from a king but he greeted a queen whose chastity, so he must have thought, had turned to ice; the queen of snow (how could he know about Remus and the queen of fire?).

"Yes, I have come to see your king. I have brought a request to him."

"Good Sister, the forest has missed you. When the twins were small, it seemed that you had come back to us, and we brought our gifts—for you as well as them. Then you left us again, more surely than at first. Have you returned for good?"

"Yes. If you will accept me."

"So late, so late. Wolf cubs have died, hunters have slaughtered deer. For want of you."

"Too late, Lordon?"

He touched my shoulder with the wisp of a finger. "Never, Good Sister. Green-O-the-Woods."

"You know his name for me."

"And why you have come."

"Will your King see me?"

"I will take you to him."

I followed him down the serpenting path

. . .into a woodland which did not seem to have grown, so surely, so perfectly did it grow, bend, curve; rather, it seemed a water greener than tourmalines and frozen in its leap: trees sweeping upward and upward and curved at the top like a great, breaking wave eternally caught in its fall; mahogany, palm, and cork; and flame tree, liquid sun at the crest of the wave.

"And where is your house?" I asked.

"There, in the underside of the wave."

"But that is a tree!"

"A monkey puzzle tree. It is very large, you see.

116

The largest in all of the world, so we think." Its roots rioted above the ground, a wonder of friendly serpents. Its multiple trunks uplifted a riot of limbs, of larger snakes, to baffle even a monkey bent on fun.

"And the houses grow from its limbs like nests."

"Follow the lift of the longest limb. There, among the leaves—a different leaf. Palm thatch. My thatch. The blue monkeys bring me my food, the wind is my broom, the tree mice clear my table of crumbs."

"You will show me the house—after we have seen the King?"

"No, Good Sister. It is not permitted."

"Am I less than one of your own race?"

"Is the grain of sand less than the mountain? Is the moon more than the luna moth? Here, there is neither more nor less. There are only differences."

"You speak in parables, Lordon."

He smiled his open, disarming smile. "But you can read them."

Then, under the green wave, forever seemingly threatened by inundation, forever shielded, a palace.

. . .

"A halcyon."

"A phoenix. The Phoenix Palace. Pagoda, we call it. A temple and palace in one, just as the smallest house is also a shrine."

The triple tiers, lessening in size, growing in delicacy, climbed on each other's backs like giant phoenixes, each projecting outward and upward its feathery points; their walls were windows like transparent wings, and atop the tallest bird sat an image which seemed a kind of enormous—

"Bumblebee!"

"No," he laughed, "though he does have a pair of wings. He is one of our temple dogs."

"But he is much too fat to sit on a flower."

"The flower, as you call it, could support a Cyclops."

"But look at his feet. He couldn't outrun a pregnant cow."

"He isn't meant to run. He sits and grins and glowers."

Squat, fanged, with long toenails and fiery red eyes, he sat, grinned, and glowered, and yet, withal, with more friendliness than ferocity. Let demons beware of him and the King he served, Lemur and Strige or whatever spirits haunted these happy folk; let friends know the grin for them, the glower for their enemies (but please, let him not need to chase!).

"The palace is built of cork. A thousand, thousand pieces carved and fitted without any need of mortar."

"But cork is brown. That much I know. I see a dozen colors."

"Brown deceives. We call it the secret color because it hides all colors—blue and red and aquamarine—and only waits for the sun to seek them out. Inside, our King sits enthroned on a teakwood chair and listens to our complaints, communes with the spirit of his great-grandmother, and dispenses justice while he takes his tea."

"And guards his treasure. I have heard——"

"Then do not ask." He smiled. "But since you have heard—I am, you see, a hopeless gossip. Secrets are terribly hard to keep, and I know so many, and you are an excellent listener, and the King never lets me talk. So . . . he guards the rarest treasure between the Pillars of Hercules and the Land of the Yellow Men; a library—palm leaves, not papyrus—preserved against dust and worm, and rich with the greatest writings of men and gods. Your own Homer's epics; a chronicle of the wandering Centaurs; the Book of Tages, the gray-haired child. . . ."

"If I could read them——"

"To some it is given to read, write, and preserve. To others, to do those deeds which ought to be preserved."

"And to you?"

"I sing. It isn't much. But then a snail isn't good for much either, is he? But he crawls, he waves his feelers and makes us laugh, he leaves behind him a silver trail and, when he dies, a pretty shell like mother-of-pearl. I should hate a world without any snails. Come, the King will meet you in the Shrine."

A slender bridge, which seemed to have dropped from the sky, rainbowed above a pool of vermillion fish and joined the steps of the palace to an islet of palm trees like green parasols, and bamboos with silver leaves, and white cranes poised on a single leg, and blue monkeys, blue flamelets, spurting among the infinite greennesses. The Shrine, a single phoenix, a fledgling with onyx wings, rose to a crimson roof where temple dogs, puppies to the guardian of the pagoda, lounged in various attitudes of fight or frolic.

We crossed the bridge as one might walk on air. The island was soft and resilient under our feet. We had stepped onto a cloud.

"The whole place," I faltered, "the bridge, the pool, the Shrine. It is———"

"Beyond words? But of course. Tishtar, the star god, helped us to build the place. He filled the pool from the Milky Way and caught the fish in the sky and painted the shrine with night's own ink and dripped the fires of Antares on the roof."

"Will you stand beside me when I meet your king?"

"You have nothing to fear, Good Sister."

"He will read my heart."

"And find it true. Yes, I will stand beside you if you like." He took my hand; I looked at the top of his hood and, sisterly, pressed his hand.

Between the bridge and the shrine, palm trees drooped with the weight of green burdens—coconuts?

"Babies!" Curled into balls, eyes closed, suspended by viny tails.

"Female Telesphori are always trees. Parent Palms, they are called. You see, our race has endured since before the Flood because we are one with the earth. We do not conquer nature, we grow with her, even as you, Good Sister. Nature abides and so do we. Males who walk, females who cling to the earth but think and dream. The trees bear fruit of themselves, but the love of the males, sweeter than wind chimes, hastens the young to maturity. Then they are plucked from the limbs and reared in the monkey puzzle tree. Always, they keep the tail, the vine, which once interlocked them with the mother tree. Did you suspect that *I* have a tail, Good Sister? I hide it under my hood, but really it is more than presentable. The female young are hardly distinguishable from coconuts. They of course are planted to sprout new trees."

He patted a trunk and pointed among the fronds. "Did you know that my bride is going to bear me a son? See? The pink nose, the tightly closed fists. Soon he will open his eyes. I sing to him every night, but not a lullaby. He likes adventure:

> He has run away.
> Look for him where the dolphins
> Mount the hooping waves
> And monkey-crowded islands
> Chatter to the pumpkin sun.

"I will bring him a natal gift," I said.

"Will you? Dearest Mellonia, dearest Green-O-the-Woods. There was a time when your people ruled the forest. They sheltered us after our long migration until we could find our own valley and grow our own trees. They showed us their healing herbs, their edible roots. Strangers, we did not feel estranged. When you became queen, we felt more than ever befriended. Until——"

"Cuckoo died. Then Ascanius. One by one my subjects fell to blight or fire or a woodsman's ax. I alone was prolonged beyond my time, my body imprisoned in spring. I alone had broken Venus' design."

"Perhaps my King can tell you about design."

"The same?"

"The same. But just as one man may see a mermaid sunning herself atop the waves, another a fat old sea-cow, so there are different ways to look."

"And who is the god of the shrine?"

"Minutius."

"But he is the god of trifles!"

"You see? To some a dwarf. To us a giant, in power if not in size. Tishtar, the star god, guided us from the East. But we wanted a local god, a god of this land. Why not Minutius? Thus, his shrine. Thus, his image. See? No hood for *him*. His purpose is plain. Protection, peace, prosperity." A boy awaiting manhood, brother to Vaticanus, he stood in brown mahogany on his pedestal: He wore the tunic familiar throughout the west: eastern slippers with upturned toes; hair in a wooden braid which almost reached the floor.

"What do you call the braid?"

"A pigtail."

"But it doesn't look like a pig's tail at all. It is much too elegant."

"Would you badmouth the pig, after all he has given you? Meat to eat from his ribs and flanks and back? Glue from his hooves? Purses from his ears? To us he is almost as sacred as a palm tree. We don't eat him, we name a coiffure for him. But here now, I mustn't tire you with accolades for the pig."

"Mellonia."

The King had crossed the bridge on silken slippers with upturned toes and clasps of black pearls. Now, removing his slippers to place them by the door, he smiled the young, artless, unworldly smile of one who watches clouds or tries to count the stars. He wore a kimona, a loose, billowing robe embroidered with scarlet poppies and caught at his waist with a wide sash. His hair, the red of a woodpecker's crest and braided down his back like that of his god, was a wonder to me who had never seen a Telesphorus without his hood. Behind him padded a large, ursine creature, plump, piebald, eminently lovable in coun-tenance and performance, a jester in fact—he wrin-kled his face, patted his stomach, and lay on his back, feet in the air, as if he were dead (but I caught him watching me through a half-closed eye).

"Mellonia," smiled the King. "My friend is known as a panda. Don't be afraid of him. The worst he will do is lick your hands."

"Afraid? I want to stroke him."

"Black and white, inharmonious harmony."

123

"A living parable," I smiled.

"Ah, you have caught the spirit of our valley. Will you drink with me?" He filled the tiny porcelain cup, eggshell blue, eggshell delicate, from a pot with a curving spout like the neck of a goose.

"It is called a teapot," he smiled. "But the drink I am serving is more akin to wine. Arak. The juice of the coconut mixed with herbs and left to ferment in the deep, cool earth." I had heard of the drink, a cathartic, not an intoxicant, to the stomachs of Dryads and men. But who can refuse to drink with a king?

He sipped, sighed with delectation, and stared into space as if he were looking for stars in the afternoon sky. Another Numitor?

"Coconut palms. Now there is a subject to tempt a philosopher. As a matter of fact, this shrine is built from the many parts of the tree. The stool on which you sit—it is woven of fibrous ropes from coconut husks. And those, my pets"—baskets cradling bonsai, diminutive trees perfect in micorocosm—"their baskets are dyed with a dye extracted from the fronds. Now. Give me your hands." He rubbed them with ointment sweeter than myrrh. "Nut-butter. It comes from the lining of the coconut shell. We use it as you use olive oil. Also for candles. You might call the coconut palm our vegetable pig. Infinitely versatile, don't you see."

I finished my cup of arak between his sentences.

"King," I said, "I have come on an urgent mission."

"Urgent, my dear? There are no sundials in the Valley. You of the West have made a god of patterns. Well, so have we. But you have made a second god of order. Everything to its time, you say. Everything to its place. Thus, thus, and thus. Bravo! A temple with four matching pillars. A poem with rhyme. Consider, however, the risk: the Fonti or fountain spirits. Perfect of face and limb, a pattern of color and configuration. But cold. Cold perfection. Better a panda, a happy confusion of night and day. Better a coconut palm, that skinny, sway-backed genii with open hands. Better a monkey puzzle tree, a sweet meandering of limbs and leaves. Climb the mountain of her tallest trunk, explore the forest of her thickest branches. At last the moon! You of the West want moons without climbs."

Dear Zeus, would he never end? *Remus a captive, Romulus ready to launch his folly. . . .*

"King—what shall I call you? I don't even know your name." If I knew his name, perhaps I could claim his attention: "Ramases, Hammurabi, Solomon, hear my request! Help me, a king to my sometime queen."

"In the West, there are names for everything. Name, count, categorize into tidy packages, tidy patterns. Ah, then comes knowledge. Ah, then comes wisdom. We of the East know what we do not know.

You want clarity. We are sometimes content to remain in mystery. The god beyond Tishtar, the sky which holds the stars, is neither male nor female, substance nor shadow. We do not try to give it a name. . . . Now, a toast to Miñutius, named by westerners who mistake him for petty because he is small." He spilled a fourth of the cup at the feet of the god. "The last is always the best."

"And I will sing a song," said Lordon. Wind chimes stirred invisibly among the trees; too melodious for bronze or gold; a gem perhaps, jade against jade, earth-green against cloud-white. They sweetened but did not muffle his sweet, small voice:

> Little, laughing lad of flax,
> Seed become a tree:
> Woodsman, wielding toothéd ax,
> Bite himself, not thee!

"Your song is not for the god, I think," said the King. "You have sung in rhyme. You have sung for our guest. Never mind, dear friend. You know her need. Mellonia, what do you ask of me?"

"What you have doubtless guessed. May Lordon's song be true for Remus."

"Do you doubt that it will?" The King was not, after all, another Numitor. I saw in his young-old face antiquities of kingliness. He had been a king when he came to the forest before the Etruscans; when I was a child. He had defended his valley from many

126

enemies. Dammed a scalding spring to drown an army of squid-eyed Cyclopes. Routed a pack of wolves with darts which were dipped in the deadly juices of the oleander. Slain an army of Gauls with a bird's nest soup, bamboo slivers hidden among the twigs.

"I am going to fight the woodsman," I said. "In spite of his toothéd ax."

"But of course. You are a queen."

"There were powers I had . . . but all things fade with disuse."

"Not your beauty," he said. "Do you think that my juices have dried with the years? Your splendors still quicken my ancient blood."

"Beauty is useless in war."

"Helen shattered Troy, in spite of Aeneas and Hector."

"There was also a wooden horse. . . . I need your help."

"But Remus is human. Not of the Forest Folk."

"I will ask what I asked of myself. 'Is he therefore less?'"

"He wishes to be a king. There are far too many kings. Their armies beleaguer our forest on every side. Etruscan, Latin, even Greeks to the south. That, I think, is why the forest appears unresponsive to you. You they remember and love—still. But he is a man. They are afraid of him. After all, those other men you loved, Aeneas and Ascanius, each of them built a city which still endures. Lavinium and Alba

Longa. The second, a hated place. Suppose the forest helps you to crown another king. And you forget—yet again—and retire to your tree to pray for sleep. What have they gained? Only the risk of another incursion, another tyranny."

"Remus will be a gentle king. The forest is in his blood. As for myself, how shall I yearn for sleep when the sweetest dream is moondust beside the sunburst of my beloved?"

"What do you ask of me? That I send my people to rescue your prince for you? We defend ourselves but we neither attack nor invade. Entreat the forest to help you as you have entreated me."

"Speak to them for me. You have never betrayed them. Say that Mellonia has returned. No, call me Green-O-the Woods."

He rose and lifted a casket of sandal wood and opened the lid. A large intaglio was its redolent heart.

"Vaticanus."

"The god of beginnings is greatly honored here. We hang his images from the parent palms. We consecrate our cradles with his name. The box is yours. So is the god."

He did not dismiss me. He forgot me to inspect his bonsai trees, addressing this one as Little Brother, that one as Moonchild, sprinkling water from a wooden sieve or bending a stunted limb into a turn of grace. He had taken arak with his guest; now he tended his plants.

"They are like his pets," said Lordon. "Cats to

Etruscans, Luperca to you. Without love, they will shrivel and die. Come, it is time to leave him alone with them."

"The panda. May I tell him goodbye?"

"He will be very hurt if you don't. Stroke his fur but not against the grain."

He lolled at my feet and leaned his head to my hand; he purred but without the sibilant hiss of a cat.

"Is he really a bear?"

"Must I classify him, Good Sister? An almost-bear, I would say. A better disposition than the altogether, though inclined to be lazy. Like me. If I tell you that he is closer to the raccoon than the bear, you will ask me to describe and classify the raccoon."

"I will ask you no such thing. Unlike the monkey puzzle tree, I am tired of meandering. Lordon, does your King mean to help me?"

"He gave you the box and the god."

"If I could have called on him in his palace. . . . A visit of state. As it was, I seemed no more than a casual guest. Less than one of his bonsai plants."

"Do you know, dear Green-O-the-Woods? In one way only are you less than the queen you were."

"And what is that?"

"You listen intently with your mind. Sometimes, though, you forget to listen with the—how shall I say?—the sap of your heart."

"I don't understand."

"He talked about patterns."

I did not need a shrine among the Wanderwood. I stretched my arms as if I could touch the sky.

"Lady of love," I pleaded, "forget my earlier prayers. Forgive my dream of the snow and the winding sheet. Make of my beauty a many-fruited palm. Phoenix, Halcyon, Woodpecker: warriors . . . builders of cities straining toward empire. I, their beloved. I, the nourishing mother? If it please your holy design. . . ."

Then the final prayer.

I took the knife from my sash—yes, I had worn it even robed as a queen—and slashed my arm.

"Mars, awaken! Father of Remus, rouse the thunders and steal the lightnings of Jove. I am your shield. Use me to guard your sons. I am your sword. Wield me to slay their foes. If it please your holy design."

I brandished the dagger like a brand.

I, a queen.

SYLVAN

I

White above Alba Longa, the temple of Vesta
glowed in the light of a quarter moon, and orange
Arcturus, the star of spring, climbed the four pillars
and the imageless pediment and seemed to poise like
a phoenix atop the roof. Fifty men—shepherds,
thieves, murderers, and one honest Faun—crouched
in the forest below the gate; fifty against a thousand
behind the walls. Romulus with the ancient sword of
Mars; I with a sling and a pouch of rounded stones;
most with hickory bows or shepherd staffs: such
against city walls, such against swords and shields.
Our battering ram was an elm tree cut in the forest;
our ladders, saplings with hempen rungs. What had
shepherds to do with Etruscan foundaries . . .
bronze and iron . . . greaves or corselets or helmets
plumed with ostrich tails?

I remembered another night, a palisade, a band of
unarmed Fauns, when shepherds were wolves or
giants, and I, their booty. Remembered, but not with
rage. A god had heard my prayer. Where was Romulus' god, almighty Mars? Behind the walls, it would
seem, bought like the mercenaries with a tyrant's
gifts.

"We can wait no longer," said Romulus. "Where is your Dryad, Sylvan? Asleep in her tree? And what can she bring us except a decrepit old wolf?" It fretted him waiting for her, a Dryad and woman; his brother's Green-O-the-Woods. It fretted him following orders from a Faun.

"But Arcturus has just now risen above the temple. Before, he was still climbing. I know she will come!"

"And what if she does? We're fools to try the gate, which seems to be her intention. We should breach the walls on the opposite side."

"There's only one gate. You know that."

"Walls, I said, not gate. Our battering ram——"

"Won't batter stone as thick as your hut."

"Scale them then."

"Hush," I snapped. Faustulus, aching in his joints, had remained on the Palatine. It was left for me to contradict the Wolf. "My ears say listen."

The inexplicable quiver, the intimation of sound before the truth: the invisible hands of the wind? The wispy step of a deer in grass and daffodils? No, it was like the hum of a distant waterfall, liquid, melodious, but imperceptibly flowing into a stream and moving through the trees, toward Romulus, toward me.

"Sylvan." The ears of a wolf are also keen. "Sylvan, it sounds like water, but it can't be. Not in these woods. I think it is——"

"Bees."

"That's how you found her, isn't it? Watching her bees!"

"Yes."

Moondusted, they whirled in a Milky Way above our heads. Bees are commonplace to a shepherd. But these . . . armed, obedient, uncountable; countless, the queens who had sent their workers to fight for a Dryad queen.

"But where is *she*?"

Romulus had his answer.

"A goddess. . . ."

"Woven of moonlight. . . ."

"No!" Only I had seen her in the tree. "The light is hers. The forest is in her, not the moon. Nothing about her is borrowed."

Green-O-the-Woods. . . . I had to guess the green, but woodscents preceded her like an armament . . . roots and bark and sap. . . . Nothing of sweetness for such a night. Tall, she seemed (though I knew her small). The surge, the thrust, the reach of a tree. Tall against storm, hard against ax's tooth. The soul of the forest was in her face. She had loved Aeneas, but he had come from a city. She had loved his son, but he had come from the sea. She had never entirely belonged to them. Count the rings in a trunk and tell its age. . . . Age was in her eyes. Study the fresh young greenness of leaves and tell their youth. . . . Youth was in the hair like a swirl of foliage around her head.

Green-O-the-Woods. . . .

133

"Her breast cups. They are silver moons!" Celer.

"They aren't cups," I bleated. "They're sheer, naked unadorned breasts."

"Naked—"

"It is the custom of Dryads. Her breasts are magic. Arrow-proof. Like Achilles, except for his heel." (Remus, forgive me the little lie.)

"Mellonia," I said, proud to speak for her; proud to speak to her.

"Sylvan! And Romulus—the tallest, the brawniest. Cub become a wolf. I cradled you once. But that was a world ago."

I had never seen him kneel, not to a god, not even beside the couch of a dying friend. He knelt to *her*.

She laughed and took his hand and raised him to his feet.

"I couldn't cradle you now, dear Romulus. Even kneeling, you remain a giant. But there is work to do. *Wait. When the gate is open, I will raise my arm.*"

"I have brought a battering ram. Ladders. . . ."

"You will soon be a king. I am already a queen."

Speechless, he watched her draw a knife from her sash and unflinchingly carve a wound above her breasts. No mere scratch. It *bled*. I had seen her work with a knife. She meant to bleed. Still, I wanted to staunch the flow.

"No, Sylvan. I know what I am about. Don't mistake me for hysterical Dido. *Helen first, then a*

134

wooden horse. Between them they toppled Troy. When the gate is open, I will raise my arm. Enter with your men."

She climbed the hill toward the gate, limping into a doll; grace departed from her; bees too, extinguishing into the blackness above her head.

"She looks like a hurt child," said Romulus. "So small. . . . What can she do without her bees or my men? See, she has started to limp!"

"A witch," said Celer. "The same, after all these years."

"Celer, will you stop babbling? Romulus, trust her. Aeneas did."

Now she was midway between the woods and the gate, climbing the basalt avenue, the Sacred way; slowly; a stricken girl. . . .

"Guards!" The call was a plea. "Help me. I am hurt." The hill, like an amphitheatre, amplified the sound. The words rang as clearly as the speech of a mime, down to us, up to the double towers. Rushlights flared in the towers.

"Help me. The wolves."

"Who are you?" Gruff; more doubtful than hostile.

"I have come from Veii. Wolves from the forest . . . overturned my carriage. Killed the driver. . . ."

The light blinked out in one of the towers. The gates sucked inward; sidewise, the jaws of a bronze Talos, the firebreathing giant of Crete. The light reappeared in the space between them, the guard with the torch. I thought, remembering a palisade: a tongue in the giant's mouth.

The guard, merely a man, stepped from between the protective jaws; moved cautiously down the hill toward the woman crying for help; saw that her wound was real, dishevelment too; saw the boldness of breast, the inhuman face, dropped his sword; anchored his torch in the ground; knelt to deity.

She raised her arm.

The guard mistook the gesture and lent his hand. Excitement made him shout—fear of the wolves, perhaps—wonder at what he had rescued from their jaws. "Yes, yes. We'll soon have you safe behind the gates!"

Romulus earned his name, though even he could not outrun a Faun.

"Sylvan," he laughed. "Rivals still?"

"Still!"

There was no more breath for speech. The hill swelled above us, black, unending, the wall of a mountainous wave. Swimmers, would we never reach its crest? We must guess the army of shepherds at our backs; trust that they did not flag.

Mellonia clung to the guard like a drowning swimmer; he struggled, lifting her, to rise from his knees; forgotten, torch and spear. Mellonia's body blocked us from his view. Also, we did not run on the road; our sandals whispered silkenly up the grass.

"Eyes like yellow moons. First they killed the horses. Disemboweled them. Horrible. Horrible."

"Yes, yes, but they are gone."

Gone?

The high, keening wail of a she-wolf . . . no one knew from whom. Not Romulus. Celer, perhaps. The army had not been trained to stealth.

"But what—but who are they?"

He looked to her for answers. Hypnotic, she held him questioning.

"Guards!" he roared, wrenching free of her. Her face spun momentarily into my view. In the light of the torch, in the fugitive light of the moon, I saw divinity, naked, terrible, beautiful. In her own tree, the time with Remus, I had seen her bemused by sleep, then angry, then repentant; I had hated her for bewitching my friend. I had called her the Squirrel. The second time in her tree, I had seen a troubled woman with many doubts and no certainties. I had called her a queen.

("Dearest Sylvan, where are my subjects? I have given myself too long to winter."

Awakened, she exulted in spring, the season of clawing roots as well as bursting buds.)

The guard had reached the gate. The bronze jaws began, implacably, to close; light dwindled between them to a thin yellow line—fire in the throat of the giant.

Another light forsook us: the quarter moon. Clouds?

"Bees!"

In a humming rain, they inundated the narrow-windowed towers, the escaped guard, the gatekeeper turning a bronze capstan; their friends we could not see. I heard no cry from them. I could only guess them dead, smothered or stung, when the yellow line remained the width of a man. Romulus first, I after him. . . .

Then, the confirmation of the guess.

I could not even call them bodies. Nothing of man remained to dignify them. Black, bloated, they affronted the blazing torches. Already they belonged to the Nether Land. I wished them quickly into Lemures—mists, chills, whatever suited them (for ghosts take many shapes).

Romulus manned the capstan. "Like a ship with an anchor!"

"Yes. Ascanius planned it. The pirate prince."

I have sometimes been drunk with Bacchus. Never, with Mars. His was the greater intoxication. A city awaited conquest; or waited to conquer. Whichever, I was drunk, triumphantly and recklessly. Romulus too. Friends in war if not in peace.

Mars made me brave when the soldier charged at me, a Cerberus hunting supper for every mouth. In truth, he seemed to brandish a dozen limbs, if only a single head. Never had I seen such a viciously slicing sword. I had no time except to count what I had to lose. Both horns in a single blow . . . left ear . . .

right ear . . . tail if he catches me from the side
(Faunus, preserve the silk!).

I raised my sling. *Quick, quick, Sylvan. Neck
comes next!*

I caught him in the teeth with my stone. His arm
made a final, futile swish. Like a broken bow, he fell
at my feet. He was the first man I had ever killed.

"Romulus," I wailed, sobered of Mars.

"Yes, Sylvan?"

"I killed a man!"

"Only one? You'll have to improve."

"Mars, come back!" I have never liked the god. He
was Remus' father, I know, but Romulus' too. Still,
Romulus was my friend in war.

The god was busy on every hand. Fifty shepherds.
A hundred soldiers, I judged (poor in numbers, I
made a round guess). Well, the space was cramped
between the gates and the town. Good for knives,
bad for swords. My territory! Sling useless, I used
those double knives, my horns. Remember, I had
trained with Romulus' men.

Someone shouted, "Get that goat!"

The goat got him.

And more—

And—

"Numitor!" Romulus raised the cry.

"Numitor is king!"

Was he king?

A graveyard of armor lay at our feet. The wearers

seemed to have shrunk into death; the armor wore
the men. We had won the gates and, unopposed,
thought we had won the town. Where were Amulius'
thousand mercenaries? Drunk? Asleep? A myth to
cow a credulous people?

"On to the palace. Numitor. Remus!"

"*Amulius!*"

A row of spears glittered across our path, like the
oars of a galley raised from the sea in sparkling unison. A row of spears to bar our advance and behind
them another, another, and finally archers, grim as
Etruscans bronzes. We had roused and routed the
garrison at the gate, a win of sorts: twice our number, mighty in armor and mightily drilled. Now we
must meet the bulk of Amulius' army. We had spent
our wind in the climb and the fight at the gate. We
had lost a dozen men (alas, not Celer). Mars, the
intoxicant, had lost his power. A cold sobriety
splashed us in the face. How could we shake those
fixed, immovable spears? Sink the galleys which
guarded the inner sea?

"Where are the bees?" cried Romulus.

"Dead, most of them. They die, you know, when
they lose their stingers."

"And the Dryad?"

"Hasn't she done her part?" I cried, furiously, because I expected more for Remus' sake, and more
she did not owe. She had opened the gates to us; to
us it remained to capture the town.

140

I heard them before I caught their scent, the padding of feet on stone, muffled as raindrops.

I caught their scent—fur, grassy and wet from the woods—before I saw them.

"Romulus, back against the houses," I cried. "Let them pass."

In the space of a single night, he had learned to take commands from a Dryad and a Faun. It was the night when he learned to be a king.

Mellonia led the pack. The light in her eyes was from the wilderness. Beyond pity or cruelty, pride or pain: Diana, ordering Actaeon's hounds to tear him into shreds.

"Sylvan!"

"Green-O-the-Woods!" Thus I allied myself with the woods and the hated wolves and Remus' rescue, whatever the cost. Inhumanity? Divinity? Names are invented by men and Fauns. When the forest wars with the town, names are meaningless except for one: inevitability.

It is said that Etruscan princes, when they hunt, bewitch the animals with the piping of flutes and lure them into their silken nets. Mellonia had such a power with wolves. She did not mimic their high, eerie wailing, their doglike barks. She sang like a musical instrument. Flute? Lyre? Cithara? No. Something to do with trees. Wind chimes, jade against jade in shaken branches. (Once, pausing above the Valley of the Blue Monkeys, I had heard such a sound. I had turned and fled from the place before I could be bewitched.) Like the wind she gently coerced them to her chosen path.

Not without help. Music and magic are not enough with wolves, mercurial, savage, tender, quick to rend, strong to defend. Luperca helped her. Where was the scrofulous old bitch who begged for milk and napped on Remus' couch? Here was a second queen! One of her subjects, a lusty male, sighted his longtime foe, a shepherd, and strayed from the pack to pursue his private war. Luperca snapped at his heels—bit them, in fact—and shouldered him into line. Queen together with queen, she advanced with Mellonia on the levelled spears, the tightening bows.

The spears wavered like oars engulfed by a wave. The wave was wolves. An irresistible tide, it obeyed the command of its own particular moons. The archers never fired their bronze-beaked birds. The taut bows dipped in their hands, momentary spears, and fell with the bowmen into a sea of blunted weapons and striving hands and, dark in the pallid light, a sea not figurative: of blood.

Soldiers reeled against doorways and beat their fists for asylum. The doors which had opened too often to hands grasping for taxes—jewels, gold, garments, food—remained inexorably closed to them. Torches flared on the flat, raised roofs. The tyrannized gathered to watch the rout of the tyrants.

"Numitor!" Romulus' cry.

"Numitor! Numitor! Numitor!"

Echoes?

Answers.

The city was won.

But the march of an army through a conquered town is like a plague through a field; it must feed and feel its way as it goes. Remus remained to win.

"Mellonia!"

A wolf snapped at my feet and found a hard hoof in his snout instead of a tender heel.

"Mellonia, we must find Remus. I know the palace a bit. Romulus never saw it. Not since he was a baby."

"Show me, Sylvan. Luperca, watch your friends." (Then, something in wolf, perhaps a queen's diplomacy, perhaps a compliment.)

In a mist of bees, we threaded the market of vari-colored stalls; canvasses, folded like morning glories for the night. Tomorrow the vintner would hawk his wine, the farmer his gourds and melons. A girl with golden baubles would sell a rarer fruit. Tomorrow, in peace!

But now was tonight.

"There is a certain god," said Mellonia. "An altar. . . . There, the small white stone. Is that it?"

"Minutius?"

"Yes, I want to say a prayer."

"Now? But he's the god of trifles!"

"I know. The prayer is small." She smiled a wisp of a smile.

The palace reflected the amber light from the

hearth in the temple to Vesta. The Etruscan lions, deserted by their guards, loomed in leonine majesty beside the broad stairs as if to invite and guide.

Momentarily, the palace seemed a bewilderment. Remember, I had seen one bare corridor and one small garden.

Three passages forced us to choose.

"Amulius was vain of his power. He wouldn't hide his throne. There will be signs——"

"That one——" Flanked by spearstands, hung with shields, it seemed to prefigure king.

"There, the pine-knot torch above the door."

"Amulius' audience room," Mellonia said.

Curule chair of Nubian ivory and smoky gold. . . . Candelabra clustered with lamps and hung from the ceiling like a constellation. . . . Mournful flickerings on the frescoed walls, a scene of revels, raised cups, spilled wine.

"Empty," I said. "No one to guide us."

"Let my bees find him."

"But I thought they were gone. Or dead."

"No. Some have followed us all the way. See?"

Bees were wavering in the open door; briefly a rectangle, they flowed into the room.

"Those are from Remus' hive. They have kept their sting." She raised her arms and inscribed the air with lines and circles, like the loopings of bees to tell the location of flowers or warn of a foraging bear.

"Did they understand?"

"Yes. They know his name. Like this." A darting

hand, fingers flaring into a flame or an outspread tail. "The Bird of Fire."

I looked at her in the light of the many lamps and caught my breath. Fatigue had youthened instead of aged her. Her face was that of a girl, pale, gaunt, bruised. I thought of a lotus blossom, newly opened and dropped into a turbulent stream.

"Mellonia, you must rest. You have been too long from your tree." I led her to the chair.

"No," she said. "Amulius sat there." She stared at the plum-colored hangings behind the chair. "Even his dye is false. Not the Tyrian purple, the colour of kings, but the dye of trumpet shells."

"Here then. Rest in my arms. Remus' friends will find him."

"I am used to comforting. Used to be, at least. It is good to be comforted. . . . It will be all right for him?"

"Yes."

"How do you know? I'm not even sure that my bees can find him."

"I too have prayed."

"Faunus?"

"Remus' god."

"Vaticanus. Then we can only wait."

The bees, returning, buzzed excitedly around my head ("Watch my ears," I hissed). I sprang on the curule chair and plucked a lamp from the candelabra. A maze of corridors awaited us under the palace: Amulius' labyrinth, cut from the living rock, moist with slime from underground streams (but where was the Minotaur?). The palace shown to the people was relatively small but bright with lamps and rich with Etruscan frescoes and tapestries. Hidden, the labyrinth stretched cell upon torture cell beneath the places of light. Eyes peered at us between rusted bars; blinked in the sudden glow of our lamp; fearing freedom, returned to nests of excrement and straw.

"Some have been in these cells for half their lives," Mellonia said. "Or so I have heard. Those who opposed Amulius when he seized the throne. They have even forgotten how to speak. One thing only do they remember: how to die. In the winter, they can eat their straw and freeze to death."

"Not only men," I said. I had caught a whiff of —other.

"The Forest Folk. The ones he uses in his circuses."

"Dear Faunus, what is *that?*"

"A Triton."

Shut from the sea, shut in a tub hardly larger than a large cask of wine, he had degenerated into his fishy elements. His chest and shoulders, once human, had become a faulty extension of his tail; a mistake. His arms were barnacled with black sores. Hair like seaweed almost obscured his face, its popped lidless eyes and sucking mouth.

"And the Centaur— He hardly has strength to

hold up his head and arms. Do you know, I never saw one in the forest."

"Because they are here in the city. They are much too big to hide. Amulius' soldiers seek them out."

"He looks so august," I said. "Somehow I expected mostly horse. Just as the Triton is mostly fish."

"Centaurs were the wizards of the forest. Even captivity can't undignify them."

Then, the final room. A fallen torch in front of the final cell. The door hung open on a leathern hinge. I thought of a house from which the thieves had fled without any plunder.

Amulius hunched like a bloated owl across the sill.

Luperca, as immovable as a guardian sphinx, commanded the cell. No, a sphinx is a kind of lion with wings, mysterious, *mixed*. Luperca was sheer and unmysterious wolf. She had killed the would-be killer of her cub.

Now, she rose to her queenliest height and bared her teeth.

For her, it was a smile.

Remus stepped from his cell, dirtier than the thief of Numitor's herd. Still, I saw no wound more serious than a cut.

"Do you know, she wouldn't let me out, even when he was dead. She thought there might be more. And once I complained of too many mothers!"

"But how did she find you?" I cried.

"Followed his scent," said Mellonia. "That's what

I told her in wolf, before we separated: 'Luperca, watch the pack unless you catch his scent. In that case, go to him at once.' "

"Yesterday, Sylvan and I walked down the main street of town. We must have left a spoor. She picked it up, followed it right into the palace. Came here. He was saying my friends had attacked his palace. Said he was going to make me his hostage. I think he meant to kill me. He knew his palace was lost. Throne too. Nothing else counted. Luperca spun him around with a well-aimed blow and went for his throat."

"Dearest Remus. Once I was proud to be your mother. Now I will leave that honor to Luperca."

He buried his face in the green intimacies, the woven secrecies, of her hair, trying, it seemed, to hide —from what? Maturity, I think. Trying to remain a boy in a dream, ensorceled from the truth about wars and death and the mortality even of kings and queens. Then, he stood to a prince's height and rocked her in his slender, manly arms. She had become the child; he, the man, he, the guardian of her, the forest's mother. I tried to enfold them into my own embrace, forgetful that love, however strong, is also brief, because it is bound by the frailties of the flesh. I tried to enfold them into magic and blunt, like a ring of shields, menacing arrows and biting axes. My stubby fingers touched but could not lock. I was a Faun, as brief as love.

"Come," I said. "We must find Romulus. He is much concerned."

We climbed the stairs at the mouth of the labyrinth.

The palace reverberated with feet, mostly sandaled, a few padded; reechoed with sounds, mostly shouts, a few yelps. Shepherds, to say nothing of thieves and murderers and an occasional wolf, are not tidy conquerors. Their shadows bristled on tapestried walls, cutthroats among heroes; their figures reeled from room to frescoed room, treasure to tantalizing treasure. A little Troy, the palace must seem to them. Aeneas' sword . . . a fan of peacock feathers . . . a pearl as big as an acorn . . . a mirror whose handle twined like mating snakes!

To the wolves, however, treasure meant food. They looked more bewildered with every room until, with Luperca's belated help, they found the kitchen, Amulius' pride, stocked with every conceivable form of edible tax. (Later, I learned that they had also found his cook, famous for pastries and poisons, hiding under a table of plucked hens. You could say that he ended his life as his own best dessert.)

"Wenches," someone was shouting. It must have been Celer. "Where are the wenches?"

"They'll come. We have the bait."

We discovered Romulus in the audience room. No, not in the curule chair. Torch in hand, he was organizing—trying to organize—a search for Remus.

"You there, Maius. Take the left wing. Maius, I say—" Shepherds had become looters, not listeners. They had fought the heroic fight and won the town. Now they were more concerned with found treasures than lost brothers, even Remus, whom they loved. When Romulus saw us, he whooped and swooped like a Gaul. Throwing his torch to me, he lifted his twin from the floor and hugged him until I had to bite my tongue to keep from shouting, "Put him down! Do you want to break his ribs?" (I fear I had grown accustomed to giving commands. The habit is easily acquired and hard to break.)

Remus' ribs did not break; in fact, he returned the embrace with equal ardor and kissed his brother's cheek. "You'll soon have a beard like Faustulus." Then, standing apart from him, he said:

"And here is Green-O-the-Woods."

The woman astonished me. Temptress, killer, lover, tired little girl, wistful beloved; mood succeeded mood; her face, the fall of her hair, the stance of her body changed like a tree, now seen at night, misty and immaterial; before the dawn, spectral with light to come; radiant with morning's larks, which are pale of themselves but catch the sunbeams as other birds catch butterflies and turn them into song; subdued at noon beneath a burst of sun; settling into a dusk with limbs outstretched as if to recall the birds—for warmth and sleep. Throughout its changes, a tree remains a tree. Its variety is not inconsistency. It stands rooted in bedrock and wonder. So too with Mellonia.

Now she was morning's tree. Radiant? Transcendent with singing larks!

The shepherds forgot their Trojan treasure.

Here was Helen.

Better,

"Green-O-the-Woods."

The voice was small and shy but clear as a cattle bell. A Telesphorus advanced cautiously but single-mindedly between the looters; he did not wish his hood to be mistaken for loot.

"I have brought you a gift, Good Sister. Rather, he brought himself. The King said, 'Take Mellonia a gift when she has won her war.' And he *would* come, in spite of everything. You'll have to grow bamboo. It's all he likes."

"But he belongs to your King!"

"No matter. A queen will do, I expect."

Mellonia opened her arms and a fat, piebald, shambling sort of a bear immediately made a lair in them. I was only glad that Luperca had gone to the kitchen to eat the cook.

II

The Fauns believe that we are born with death for a twin. We do not recognize him for many months

151

(years for a man). Fitfully, we come to glimpse and then ignore his shadow. The sun's deceit, we think, a mote in the eye. But at the last we must confront his daily presence and know him to be our mortal enemy.

I felt him in the audience room, more than a shadow, though invisible. I could not tell if he belonged to me or Remus or another man. (Not Remus, please, I thought. He already has his twin. He has just become a man, not yet a king. It is much too soon.)

Selfishly, I did not want to outlive him.

Other presences in the room were many and visible. They did not leave me time to brood. Like one returning home, Romulus had claimed the curule chair.

"Gold and ivory. Bronze would suit us better, eh, Remus?" (I was glad of the "us"; his posture said "me.") "We'll have a double throne. Side by side——"

"Brother."

"Yes?"

"Has anyone seen our grandfather?"

"By Mars' holy spear. . . ."

We went to look for the King.

His room was a welter of unwound papyrus scrolls with curious markings—an eclipse of the moon, the constellation Gemini, symbols I could not read. A tall, three-legged stool stood like an island among the scrolls. I could picture him as a fisherman atop the stool, fishing the water to catch a papyrus and interpret its stars while kingdoms glittered Venus-like from the primal foam, strung with their garlands of myrtle and bitterweed, and sank, ungarlanded, with Apollo's brazen chariot.

We found him, however, asleep on the couch, beside him the Babylonian lenses with which, between his naps and studies, he watched the stars in the sky. His white beard inundated his blue coverlet. He looked as old and august as foamy-bearded Proteus, magician of the sea, at the end of the Golden Age. He had slept throughout the fall of the city, swordplay, shouts, screams, and assorted ululations, and now he thought himself in a dream when Remus took his hand and said, with quiet affection,

"Grandfather, I have come back."

He blinked a tentative smile. "My brother let you go?"

"Your brother is dead." Briefly he described the battle, Mellonia's wolves, Romulus' valor, and my—what did he say?—sagacity. I must remember the word.

"Sylvan, you say? A splendid chap. I said when he jumped the walls, 'You can't beat a Faun for tricks.' As for my late brother, I cannot pretend to mourn him. Gemini—they stood across his horizon with boots of bronze. I warned him often enough."

"And this is your other grandson, Romulus."

Romulus knelt and kissed him on the cheek. The kneel was casual; the kiss, perfunctory.

"Grandfather, we have returned your city to you."

"Indeed? I did not know that it was gone. Only misplaced." Clearly he did not like this muscular giant, introduced to him as Remus' twin but smelling of wolves and blood. "Remus, my son. The odor of beast is very strong in the room. Goat?" He looked from me to Romulus and levelled his eye like an arrowhead. "No, wolf I think."

"And this is Mellonia. Green-O-the-Woods."

"By Saturn's beard, a Dryad in the flesh. There was such a one in Aeneas' day. But you are much too young. Scarcely older than my own Rhea. You may kiss me, my dear."

Her tact was as exquisite as her kiss. "For a great king, a tiny gift."

"The manner of giving is half the gift." He recovered Remus' hand. "My people helped you, I have no doubt. Did many lose their lives?"

"A few," said Remus, "though all were very brave." (Yes, behind their doors.)

"Take me to them."

On the roofs of the houses, the townspeople huddled like a gaggle of geese. They honked and fluttered at the sight of their king restored to them but gooselike remained on the roofs. Perhaps their hesitation was forgivable. In Mellonia's absence, the wolves had mistaken the streets for a forest. They urinated indiscriminately between cobblestones and over altar stones. They dined at leisure among the fallen bodies and peered hopefully at those unreachable delicacies atop the roofs.

No one as yet seemed ready to risk a descent. Except Balbus, the amiable dormouse. He lowered a wooden ladder and vacated his roof without any need for a balancing tail. I believe he genuinely liked the twins and welcomed Amulius' overthrow; also, his master Tullius, the second richest man in town, could be expected to fall with the tyrant. Balbus wanted to bounce.

"The herds are yours," said Romulus, expansive with other men's property. Balbus became a beaver instead of a dormouse. If he had owned a tail, he would have thumped it on the stones.

Between the guardian lions, a lordly Romulus presented Numitor a kind of votive offering, an image in stone, from the liberator to the liberated. He raised his grandfather's hand into the air; the hand did not help in the ascent; raised, it had to be held.

"Peoples of Alba Longa, your tyrant is dead. Your rightful king is restored to you!" I will have to say for Romulus that he did not make a speech, though he must have noticed the girl with the golden bangles looking at him as if he were Mars. He was eager to move to more important matters; for example, a prompt abdication in favor of youth.

With the slight but obstinate shake, Numitor recaptured his arm and faced his people. He was proud; he was paternal; he was, I feared, ready to make an interminable speech.

"Pack the old man off to bed," muttered one of Romulus' shepherds, not Celer, "and bring on the virgins." Celer would have said "wenches."

I watched Romulus' face, the lupine smile unable to hide his impatience. Remus stood at the old man's elbow, ready for instant but unobtrusive support. Mellonia? Gathering wolves as a shepherd gathers sheep. The panda—that was the name of the fat, shambling animal—had achieved a slow but resolute waddle behind her and ahead of Luperca's snappish jaws. I was pleased to see that she had released the Centaur from his cell beneath the palace. He cantered beside her, the sap of the forest already swelling in his six limbs; a wizard returning from exile. He looked, as Numitor tried to look, both proud and wise.

Remus saw Mellonia too and together we read her wistful smile of farewell:

"Tomorrow."

"She is tired," I whispered. "She wants her tree."

"I know," he said. "But she looks so small and pale. She seems to have lost her power." It was true; she had become the tree at noon, bereft of birds.

"She doesn't want you to see her like this." Presumptuous Sylvan: never in love but giving his friend advice about a beloved.

He had to stay in the town; he could not forsake

his brother at their joint triumph. Mellonia had not forsaken them; she had simply effaced herself and her army and left the occasion to the twins.

"So small and pale. . . ."

"People of Alba Longa," Numitor began in a clear, resonant, almost sprightly voice. "Amulius is dead." An artful pause, a thunder of approbation. "Alba Longa lives." A veritable thunderstorm. "My lost grandsons have returned to me." He looked pointedly at Romulus; regretfully at Remus. "A staff in my old age, they will help me to live out my years and to *rule wisely if only for a little while.* The stars foretell an auspicious reign for them in the town which they are destined to build on the Palatine." Stars, like Hades! The old man did not want sweaty, rowdy, wilful Romulus in Alba Longa. To Remus he would have yielded his throne, I think (regretfully). But he must have foreseen the unlikelihood of an equitable rule between two such diverse brothers. Star-gazing had not blinded him to the obvious. "As King of Alba Longa, I hereby declare an amnesty to all who supported Amulius, except for those loathsome ruffians, those mercenaries bought with ill-gotten taxes, who have, I see, already left our streets." (Left? Dead, every one of them. They had earned their pay.) "I will end my reign with peace, even as I began it. The years between, like the scaly winged dragon which sometimes eclipses the moon, have dwindled or passed." He paused, I should say posed, and lifted his arms with the studied flourish of an orator. A King, it seemed, even in exile, never forgot the gestures of royalty.

Thunder and lightning, rain, snow, and hail! Why not? In the past, he had never imposed, he had permitted; if permissiveness had allowed a tyrant to seize the throne, it promised now a respite, a redistribution of ill-gotten taxes among a different group of ill-getters. An older Numitor would doubtless watch more constellations in the sky and fewer manipulations on the ground.

"Long live Numitor!" (He would outlive *me*.)

"King of Alba Longa!" (He could have the place.)

The people at last forsook their roofs—the wolves by now had followed Mellonia and her fat bear out of the town—and thrust their way through Romulus' men to the feet of their king. The pliant girl, despairing of Romulus, flung her golden bangles to Numitor. Balbus bowed a repentant head (a beaver with plans). Remus clasped a restraining hand on his brother's shoulder. Romulus struck his fist against an Etruscan lion (less than bronze could not have withstood the blow). Muffled by the crowd, a susurration, like one of those tremors which anticipate a Vulcanian rage, rumbled among his shepherds. We had rescued Remus; for me, enough. We had toppled Amulius; for Remus, almost enough after his first disappointment. But the shepherds, thieves, cutthroats, and Romulus wanted the town. Build on the Palatine? They were not by nature builders—consider their squalid huts—they wanted houses already built for them, and women to wive and wench.

"Will you help me to bed, Remus?"

He did not need help; he was good for the night. But a wise orator knows when he has received his best ovation. "Tell the men the largesse of the palace is theirs. The wines, the fruits, the venisons." (He did not know about Luperca's depredations.) "Tomorrow I will resume my rule with your help. Now I will sleep."

No mention of stars.

Romulus, Remus, and I talked in a quiet garden. The conquerors, finding the kitchen impoverished of its last sausage, had joined merrymakers in the town, followed the girl without the golden bangles, returned, disgruntled, to the Palatine; in short, gone their own ways. The jonquils, golden goblets by day, had paled into ivory and seemed to be spilling moonlight into the pool.

Celer was absent from our council.

"Wounded?" I asked hopefully, thinking wolf.

"Not a scratch. You know him. Chasing a wench, I expect."

"While others play, we make plans." I thought of the pliant girl.

"Did you see Numitor's excitement?" cried Romulus. "Before he dies, it would be just like him to name another heir."

"And no park for the animals," said Remus. "He

doesn't like wolves. Bears either, I suspect. He hardly noticed Mellonia's panda." (For once I stood with Numitor.)

"Even if we stay in the palace with him," Romulus fretted, "a staff in his old age, we can't have our way in Alba Longa. What can we accomplish while an old man holds the throne? His people will not accept changes as long as he lives. They have had a tyrant; now they want an antiquated figurehead. Let them have what they want. We will build our city on the Palatine. Already we have a circle of huts. Next, we'll add a wall, then a temple to Mars, then a place of government——"

"And a shrine to our mother," said Remus, kindling to the plan. "A temple to Rumina. Another to Vaticanus, an arbor trained into a dome."

"And one to Minutius."

"Who? Oh, the little fellow. Very well, Sylvan, and a park for the birds as well as the animals. Mellonia will help us to choose the proper trees. Shady but not edible. I think, though, Romulus, that the Palatine is not the best hill. True, there are huts already. But some of the owners are thieves and cutthroats, as you well know. Let them keep their huts, but in our new city there will be no room for such men. Why not build on the Aventine? It is almost as high, and closer to the forest, to Mellonia and her friends, who won us our victory."

"Ask Father Mars who won our victory," said Romulus. "Mellonia helped, it is true. She opened the gates. She brought us the wolves—she and Luperca together. But my shepherds, Remus, captured the city. They and the men you choose to call thieves and cutthroats."

"Men like Celer make good warriors," Remus granted. "But not good citizens. I mean no disrespect to the man. But Romulus, can you see him worshipping in a temple or sitting in a senate house? Give him a woman and herds, but leave him on the Palatine. Build our city on the Aventine!"

"Ask for a sign from the heavens," I interrupted. The gods, I thought, should favour Remus. Romulus only worshipped Mars. "Consult a sheep's liver—mind you, a sheep I say—as the Etruscan augurs do, or watch for birds of good omen."

Romulus gave me one of those looks which used to say, better than words: "Goat Boy, bleating again?" This time his look did not show him a boy.

"Oh?" he said, noncommittal but not dismissing.

Remus seized his hand. "Listen to Sylvan. The Fauns, you know, taught the Etruscans divination." (He was mistaken; their god Tages taught them the art. But Fauns are so often unjustly denigrated that I allowed them to be unjustly accoladed).

"Brother, we have a lifetime in which to build and rule. Why not start from the ground?" There was dirt on his face; a bruise on his cheek; cobwebs in his hair. He showed his night in the cell. Romulus must have seen his fatigue. He could be a bully, I grant, but also a gentle nurse.

"Very well. We shall ask for a sign. Early one morning—the best time for omens—we shall climb our respective hills and watch the sky for vultures, the birds of good omen. Whoever sees the most shall choose his hill for the city. Now, Brother, let us sleep before we quarrel."

"Vultures?" I objected. "Why not magpies? They're luckier. Prettier too. Why not——?"

"Vultures are more kingly."

The palace abounded in couches. Among his more pleasant vices, Amulius had cultivated orgies. I chose a couch which, intended no doubt to be intimate for two, remained spacious for one, and dreamed of good-omened vultures (but what was the four-legged shadow which fell across my dream?).

MELLONIA

When I was a child, the youngest Dryad in the Wanderwood, my mother said that two days of every year, even more than the festival of Saturn, must always be remembered and celebrated: my birthday and the planting day of my tree.

"The tree was planted by Saturn himself," she said. "Count the rings and you will know the day." Her hair was a mossy softness above her gracefully pointed ears. Her eyebrows, however, were jagged lightning flashes instead of crescent moons. Her softest look held the hint of a thunderstorm.

"But nobody can count the rings in a tree without cutting down the trunk!"

"Child, child, the tree is your father. Mine too. Do you think he can hide his rings? Indeed, he may try, but Dryads are seers. We can peer inside of secrets, like looking into a Sibyl's cave." She closed her eyes; the eyebrows flickered their dangerous fires. "I see— One thousand and three, one thousand and four, one thousand and five. There. He would like me to forget to look. He thinks he is terribly old. Well, he is. But years should be worn with pride, like a nest of nightingales or a mantle of first-fallen snow. Every year a victory over brushfires and axes and blight."

"Back to birthdays, Mother. When is mine?" Fathers who did not speak to me were not my concern.

"Today."

"And you never told me before."

"The eleventh year. It is when you become *harmonious*. Before then, you are a single lyre note seeking a harvest song."

"How will we celebrate?"

"A party, I think, Your Aunt Segeta and——"

"Bounder." He was a Centaur boy. "Can he come into the tree?"

"You shall have to go out to him. He is much too ungainly to enter a tree. Six limbs! You may take him a garland strung with eleven chrysanthemums, and he will say, 'Mellonia, this must be your birthday. What would you like for a gift?'"

"To live forever."

"Don't make a wish in haste. You might get it."

The twin lightnings could not discourage me. "You said I could wish for anything."

I remembered the two days until Cuckoo died. Then, I hated them. Then I learned to forget them.

The second remembering was like scraping moss from a stone: suddenly, the clean, moonbright face. Today was my four hundred and eighty-eighth birthday. I was glad that my best friends had promised to visit my tree. I wore a tunic of silk chrysanthemum petals, a golden rain, and a green sash like a wisp of vine, and a cricket of black jade between the terraces of my hair.

"Remus and Sylvan! What have you brought me?"

"Why, nothing," said Remus. For him, a blush was a universal pinkening from the tips of his ears to his sandaled toes.

"Flaxen hair and a blush," I said. "Silken tail and horns like mother of pearl. What could be better for a birthday gift?"

"Birthday?" he cried. "Not enough. Here. This isn't either."

"An Adonis pot," said Sylvan, disagreeing. "I baked it."

"And I planted the bamboo shoot. Lordon brought it to me from a parent plant. In time, the shoot will make a plant of its own. It's for what's his name."

"Bounder. After my old friend, long dead."

"Pandas aren't named Bounder," said Sylvan. "That's a horse's name. Or a Centaur's. Possibly a sheep dog's. Besides, he's too fat."

"Hush, you'll hurt his feelings. If we call him Bounder, he may come to suit the name." At the moment, he looked as if he had sprouted from the ground, like a big mushroom. His day alternated between naps and meals, including, perhaps, an exercise in stealth.

"Remus," cried Sylvan. "Watch the pot! Hades, he's eaten our gift. Oh well, Remus. We shall have to find another. Now, I had better be going."

"Why?" I asked.

"Why?" asked Remus.

"I expect you want to make love."

"You Fauns," I laughed. "We don't have to *make*

love. Not every day. It doesn't fall down like a pig sty in a breath of wind."

"We only have to *be* love," said Remus.

Sylvan leaned on a single hoof; rocked, deliberated. "Two's company, three's an orgy."

"Then we shall have an orgy." I took each of them by the arm. Remus had arms like eloquent silences. Sylvan had arms like bursts of merry chatter. "It's my birthday, and that means I can do anything I like, even give presents."

"Not *him*," said Sylvan, eying Bounder. "We haven't room in our cave. What with Luperca and all. Temperamental, you see. Old. Can't stand crowds."

"Oh, I wouldn't give Bounder away. He was a gift to me from the King!"

"No wonder he's a king," said Sylvan. "If he gives gifts like that, he must keep all the treasure for himself."

My kitchen was unexplored country for Remus and Sylvan (whenever you make a new friend, everything is unexplored country. Together you draw maps). Round, windowless, it glowed with bamboo lanterns hung like moons, gifts from the Telesphori. My stove was a bronze Telchin, one of those ant-like workers who toil in the forge of Vulcan. Six bronze legs; flat top above rounded body, holding a pot as an ant holds a seed on his back; oven in head with shelf like a sliding tongue to catch my unbaked loaves.

"Herbs," said Sylvan, pointing his hoof at a ring of pots; my oaks in miniature.

"An herbarium," I said. "The lanterns are special, you see. Little moons which make things grow without sun."

"Rosemary, parsley, thyme, sage, wintergreen," said Sylvan. "Each in its separate pot. Already dished, as it were, for supper. Or late breakfast. Or simply to have on hand if company calls."

"You're as bad as Bounder," said Remus. "At least let them grow up!" He examined the room with a scrupulous eye; that of a sculptor, a poet, a mariner —in short, anyone who wonders and wants to remember. (Romulus had the eye of a warrior—anyone who hates and wants to remember.)

"It's so ed-, uh, amiable," said Sylvan.

Amiability lay in the table of lemon wood from Carthage (the spirits of citrus trees resemble haughty courtesans; their perpetual boast is the fragrance of their blossoms. I did not hesitate to borrow their wood.) Amiability lay in the three-legged, lemon-round stools, fruit of the mother table.

Sylvan sat on a stool and leaned precariously on one leg and Remus watched him to prevent a spill.

"First the gifts. Then the feast."

"Honey cakes! Pomegranate wine!" Remus, not Sylvan. Sometimes he forgot that he was a manly eighteen, a prince, a soon-to-be builder. Sometimes he was six.

"Quiet," said Sylvan. "Do you want that overstuffed excuse for a bear to hear you and invite himself to the party and hog the gifts?"

"Can a bear hog?" asked Remus.

"Well, bear gifts then."

"Bounder can't climb this high," I reassured. "He gives out in the houseplace. Usually he lies in the shade. Abides, you might say."

"Freeloads," muttered Sylvan.

I had baked the cakes to resemble trees. Tree cakes. "Oak, elm, hickory . . . And this is a monkey puzzle tree. I saw one in the Valley of the Blue Monkeys."

"It makes a big cake, doesn't it? All those corners too. Esculent convolutions, as it were."

"The one I saw was a large and inesculent convolution. They say that when a monkey starts climbing, he climbs on faith. If he isn't persistent and curious, he gives up. If he is, he gets to the top and then he can see the moon."

"Climbing a monkey tree is like building a city, I expect," said Remus. "When you start building, you can't see the end. You think whatever plan you had got lost."

"But you keep on building, like the monkey climbing, and finally you finish the design. Discover the moon. Remus, when will you choose your hill?" A Dryad's birthday may also have a design.

"Tomorrow. Early in the morning Sylvan and I will climb the Aventine and watch for vultures. If I win——"

"Yes, Remus?"

"You shall wear a crown before the earth is purified."

"I shall have to return here at night. Always. I belong to my father tree as well as to you."

"Come in the day then and sit between us, Romulus and me."

"A queen isn't divisible, Remus."

"You don't like him, do you?" He never understood why anyone could prefer him to his brother.

"I don't dislike him. I fear him. He is a force of nature. I don't want to be in his valley when he erupts."

"Romulus blusters and people think him a tyrant. Underneath, he's kind and generous."

"For you, I hope he may always be kind. Your heart is single and undivided. Like the cella of a temple, it holds no crevices for spider or worm; only the image of your guiding deity, love. Now. Your gifts."

I had woven a tunic for Remus; sleeveless and falling below the thighs and above the knees; linen but looking as if it were sewn from rushes and leaves.

"Romulus is a giant, but muscle-bound. You are a sapling. He will run to fat in his old age. Age may gray but never thicken you. Show your splendid trunk, the lean, lithe limbs. I will close my eyes while you change that poor threadbare thing———"

"Faustulus sewed it."

"I thought it might have been Luperca."

169

He was touchingly modest even with me. He never believed in his own beauty.

"There. Now you are part of my tree. Green leaves, green tunic. You carry the forest with you. Like Sylvan with his hooves and pointed ears."

"But it's too fine a gift. It's your birthday, not mine."

"My birthday, yes. The day to do whatever I please. And it pleases me to give you a tunic. And Sylvan. For you I've made——"

"A loin cloth," he sighed.

"No. I've decided I like you as you are."

"Bareflank?" he asked, incredulous.

"Bareflank. But the horns need embellishing, don't you think? Something to set them off."

"Faun bells! I didn't know anyone remembered."

"I remember what Remus told me. In the Golden Age, Fauns were the kindest folk in all the forest. Not only were they friends of the Centaurs but they rescued travelers from wolves and storms. If you needed their help, you listened for the sound of their bells and called out to them, 'Silver Bells, bring me your valiant hooves!' "

I hung them around his horns, wind chimes whose music came from silver chiming against crystal and also from the finer reverberation of silver against horn.

"Sylvan," said Remus. "You look like a king. If I were a traveller, I would call you Silver Bells. I will anyway."

A birthday was giving presents. A birthday was thinking my heart a Pandora's Box of mischief and hurt, with hope like a lost and huddled bird; then, finding a bird of fire.

"Niece, I am cold."

"I know, Aunt Segeta. Truly I do."

"Oh yes, you know now that you are warm with your precious young prince. Haven't you a little warmth to spare for one of the homeless in the Nether Lands?"

For answer, I tried to hug her. The mist of her left a dampness on my cheeks; my hands held slime. I felt as if a large wet fish had struggled out of my arms.

"I will fix you a plate of lentils and beans."

"If that's the best you can do."

"Aunt, you know it's all you can eat."

"It will do." She watched my preparations with a restless smouldering. "You have a lover. What do I get? Beans!"

"You wanted me to have a lover."

"That was before I knew how envious I would be."

"Dear Segeta," I said, "I love you very much." My protestations embarrassed her. She evaporated before she had eaten a single bean.

Suddenly I understood the Nether Land and its Lemures. Its multitude of grays, its multitude of nots. Hills instead of mountains. Streams instead of rivers. *The land of the undaring.*

Except for Remus, I too might have begged for warmth and settled for lentils. Except for Remus. . . .

The next morning I awoke to the piping of a flute, a thin silvery sound, like the voice of the rain. It was, however, a day for the sun, which had made of my window a round yellow haze. Still, I did not resent the flute. A Faun, perhaps, remembering revels in the light of a festival moon. I would share my sun.

The flutist was not a Faun; he was Lordon, kneeling among the jonquils in my altar place. I could barely see his head, his small pink fingers lifting a silver flute. Behind him I saw two of his friends. Their bodies were hidden among the flowers; their faces, muffled by hoods. But I knew them together with Lordon for the bringers of gifts and wishes to the infant twins, after the river and the osier boat.

"Lordon," I called. He did not appear to see me in my tree or hear my call. The voice of the rain was not for me. He had piped for Bounder's ear. Departing, the animal seemed to lose his play. Black and white, a walking parable, he followed the three green hoods among the trees. From the back, the hoods resembled rounded gravestones. I thought of a city whose luck departs to the piping of a sorrowful flute.

I refuse to be sad. Bounder, sated on bamboo shoots, will surely return to me. No true king would recall his gift. I will wait for Remus and news of his hill. Good news. Venus and Mars, Aeneas' mother and Remus' father, surely predestine a second Troy, and greatness does not lie with Romulus on the Palatine.

I will bake fresh cakes for the planting day of the new city.

Listen! Steps in the woods.

A birthday and a planting day in a row, like two friends. Like Remus and Sylvan.

SYLVAN

I

Numitor lost no time in approving the brothers'
plan to build on the Tiber. He gave them his own
herds, including the listless cow whose theft had
started the war, and promised workers and tools as
soon as they chose their site.

"Build with my blessing," he said. "Gemini augurs
well for you. So too do the Etruscans. I had a deputa-
tion from Veii this morning. The king likes you, Remus. He said . . . I forget what he said. Something
about banqueting in Elysium. Well, kings must have
their mysteries."

He returned to his Babylonian lenses.

At sunrise, six days after the capture of Alba
Longa, Remus and I fumigated his herds on the Palatine with sulphur to exorcise unwelcome spirits (for
even cows have their jealous Lemures) and scattered
the stalls with arbute boughs, beloved by the goats,
and wreaths of myrtle and laurel, pleasant to sheep.
It was the festival day of the Pales, the patron gods
of the herd. A fortunate day, one would think, for
shepherds to choose a hill. But fortune for whom?

With the silence of happy comradeship and high expectations, we climbed the Aventine. Our hill was a gentle Palatine; its slopes less precipitous, its mount less rugged; its grassy mounds inviting temples, markets, houses instead of walls and towers. Wild fig trees? A grove for Rumina. A rock in the shape of a cradle? A natural altar for Vaticanus.

"I wonder why the gods like vultures," I said, wrinkling my nose. I pictured the birds at a feast. "Ugh. Such ugly creatures."

Remus laughed. "Ugly yes, but helpful. They rid the forest of carcasses. And they never kill."

"Which way will they come?"

"They may not come at all. They are very rare in this country. Mellonia says to watch the river, where the animals go to drink and die. I wish she were with us."

He had seen her daily since the capture of Alba Longa. Her name was a conjuration even to my long ears, sweeter than tree cakes or Silver Bells. I had shared death with her; we loved the same friend. How could we not be friends? (I loved her next to Remus. Always, there were only the two of them. I never knew the god who envied me.)

"But how will Romulus know if we really see the number we say?"

"He will take our word," said Remus, surprised.

"And you will take his?"

"Of course."

"It means a lot to him to build on the Palatine."

In spite of my reformation, I came from a race of accomplished liars. I could spy the aptitude in kindred spirits, and Romulus struck me as apt.

"Remus, have you ever thought of building your own city—without Romulus? It won't be easy to rule with him. If you win your hill, it will be even harder. And men like Celer, how will you keep them out? Or make them behave if they enter?"

"I'll build with Romulus or not at all. He's my twin. Do you realize, Sylvan, I shared the same womb with him? The same osier boat in the Tiber. We have never been apart."

"I know, I know. You love him next to Mellonia."

"He is one of three. You, Romulus, Mellonia. There isn't a first or a last. Mellonia is someone beyond me, an image of ivory and malachite. And yet she lifts me up beside her, without seeming to stoop. You, Sylvan, are someone close and warm and familiar. A fire on a cold night. Barley loaves baking on the hearth. You never judge me. With you I am most myself. And Romulus? The stone pillars of a temple. Hard things, yes. But strong and needed."

"You are very different from Romulus. He is not always a pillar. He is"—I paused, wishing to warn, not wound—"rash in some ways."

"I know," he sighed. "And I try to temper his rashness. In return, he gives me courage."

"Courage, Remus? You have enough of your own. I never saw you hesitate when you knew what was right."

"You can't see my heart. It leaps like a grasshopper sometimes! Romulus, though, is fearless."

"You are braver then. You must conquer fear, while Romulus' courage is thoughtless, instinctive, that of a wolf."

"Sylvan, do you know you are talking bull?"

"Goat," I corrected.

Then we saw them: High above the easy orange twinings of the Tiber, six vultures lumbered toward the north and Romulus on his northern hill. Ungainly birds, hideous even at such a height—I had not changed my view—but oh, how welcome to us who counted them.

"Remus, we've won! Even if Romulus sees them, we saw them first. They are flying toward and not away from him."

We scrambled down the hill so nimbly that I thought my hooves would leave the earth; we gamboled more than climbed.

"Slow down, Woodpecker," I shouted. "Your tunic has given you wings."

He laughed and tore me a linen leaf from his waist. "Catch my feathers and fly!" (I could read his flying thoughts: roads, canals, aqueducts, parks for his animals opening into the forest. . . .)

Then, the Palatine. . . .

In a flurry of pig-trampled leaves and white dust, we skirted the circle of huts and found Romulus, waiting with Celer and several other untidy friends, on the highest part of the hill.

"Six of them," Remus cried. "Romulus, we saw six at once!"

The early light was kind to Romulus' face; it did not show the wolf.

"So did we. Just before you came." I noticed his beard, no longer an intimation; a small black *v* on his chin. The ambitious boy, impatient but having to wait, had hardened into a man who, ambitions within his sight, had ceased to wait.

"It must have been the same six. They were flying this way."

"No matter. They still count."

"Then we are tied."

"No," said Celer. "We have seen *twelve*." He imposed a smile on his mouth which looked like the grin of a mime: slash of orange on wood.

"Twelve? There have never been so many near these hills!"

"Today there were. The six that just passed, and before them, six more. Even larger—as big as eagles. They circled twice to be sure we saw them. Sent by Mars, eh, Romulus?"

Romulus frowned. "Of course it is true. Celer has just told you. And the city is mine to build where I choose."

Remus looked like a child whose parents have told him their first lie. Hopefully he waits; hopeful to hear it recalled, revised, explained. Then, the slow but irrevocable judgment of young innocence upon old guilt. "Come on, Sylvan. Let's go to the cave."

Romulus barked commands as if he already wore a crown. "Find me a bull and a heifer. We will plough the boundaries of our new city. But first, the festival of the Pales! Celer, break out the wine. And the rest of you, build us some bonfires."

After the feast, he would yoke the animals to a bronze-tipped plough and drive them around the base of the hill where he meant to build his walls, leaving unbroken ground only for the gate. The space enclosed by the plough would be "fortunate"—protected by fortune from evil spirits—and the man who dared to cross the furrow instead of entering by the designated gate would shatter the luck of the builders and, himself the first invader, encourage further invasion by animals, spirits, and men.

After the feast. . . .

Remus did not speak until we had reached the cave and he had buried himself in the deeper cave of his pallet, Luperca beside him, the ancient mother guarding her young.

"Build your own city like I said."

"No, I will help Romulus. But first I must understand him."

"Your hill was the best."

He looked at me with level, wounding eyes. "The hill is not important. Romulus lied. That is important. He is building his city on a lie and the men know."

"No one objected. They liked the Palatine."

"That is the harm. They knew and said nothing."

I left him in the cave with Luperca. At endings and beginnings, mothers and not friends are the best company.

"Rumina," I said, more in conversation than prayer. "Your tree stands right at our door. Neglect the lambs for awhile and help my friend."

In the afternoon, I climbed her tree and caught a treasure of honey in a round clay bowl. The bees did not sting me. Before Alba Longa, it was only Remus they trusted to enter their hive.

I invaded the cave like a guardian genius.

"Eat it," I snapped. "You have brooded enough."

Wordless, he tilted the bowl to his lips and drank the honey as if it were milk. He knew the gift of his own bees.

"More?"

"No," he smiled. "Now I will help Romulus with his walls. But first I want to see Mellonia."

"I'll wait for you here."

"No, come with me."

"You must have things to say in private. Who wants a Faun's big ears at such a time?"

"She has grown to love you. Besides. . . ." Can a smile, like a voice, diminish into an echo? "I want you with me. It is something I feel—a fear, a loneliness—I am not sure what. I want you with me."

The woods were mute with the spring stillness which comes of too much work: Roots toil, leaves thrust, wrens build nests, then they must sleep before they return to their work, the cycle of seasons, the pattern of day and night, sun and shade. In such a silence, Celer and two of his friends exploded like revelers at a funeral. I recognized the friends; the wife killer and the despoiler of temples.

Celer was thrashing the undergrowth with a staff; the friends stood ready with raised boots. The three of them reeked with wine—the blackberry wine of shepherds; pomegranate too, sweetly acrid to smell or taste.

"Celer!" I called. A frightened rabbit fled for the deeper woods.

He forced a grin. "Big Ears and Woodpecker. Missed our festival. Mars will be hurt."

"Do you mean the Pales?" asked Remus. "Mars is my father. I did not know that I had dishonored him."

"Remus," I said, watching them make for the Palatine with the speed of sober men. "Do you think they found her oak? Celer asked me where it was. I didn't tell him, of course. But the night of the wolves, remember, she went to her tree and Celer disappeared."

"I remember," he said. We began to run. I needed wings instead of hooves. Still, I did not let the space of his shadow fall between us. Shadows were not my friends.

In the sun-dappled haze of afternoon, in the Wanderwood, Mellonia's oak disported its branches like a god-built Troy without any obvious plan except the hill of its trunk; temples and palaces, colonnades, arches, and altars to gods of the sky mingled in artless order. I saw no hint of assault, except . . . should the word be "disorder"?

At the foot of the trunk, we paused to catch our breaths and peer above our heads.

"That lowermost branch," said Remus. "I think it is starting to wilt."

"Too little sun?"

The happy towers had lost more than their sun. Their shadows were not of the afternoon; they were blight and decay, a blackness like the heavy sandal marks of a premature frost.

"Green-O-the-Woods!" he name reechoed among the oak trees like a lost incantation.

"No sign of fire or ax. They can't have climbed the trunk either. Much too broad."

"The altar—"

Ruinous, it scattered its lesser ruin amidst broken flowers and bleeding roots. The jonquils' gilded goblets had spilled their wine. Spiny acanthuses tumbled like broken shards. Forgotten banquetings, they seemed. Revels, remembered imperfectly from the Golden Age. The men had despoiled instead of searched; still, they had found the door. . . .

Room rose above room, houseplace, kitchen, bedroom; ruins now, ruin upon ruin.

In the houseplace, they had smashed the Adonis

pots and ground the poppies and asphodels into the reeds of the floor. The tawny chair was a legless lion.

"Why do they hate flowers?" I cried.

"Not just flowers."

"Growth?"

"Because they are—stunted."

In the kitchen, they had drunk pomegranate wine and eaten tree cakes. The herbs, of course, they had strewn across the floor: roots curling like the toes of dead babies; leaves clutching at unresponsive air.

We found Mellonia on the floor beside her couch, a white stillness blighted like her tree and cradled, incongruously, among the chrysanthemum petals of her birthday robe. Remus lifted her onto the couch and smoothed her torn hair.

She opened her eyes and kingdoms stared at us—Troy, athwart her windy hill. . . . Carthage, black, buildings between a jungle and an unreturning sea. . . . A city in search of a name to bestride the world; bent upon labors, wars, glories like Hercules; a giant but blind, except when he chose to see. . . .

"Remus."

Momentarily she returned to us; a visitor, soon to be a voyager, waxing her ears against the Siren call until she had said goodbye. Barque in the copper bay, wind swelling the hyacinthine sails. Someone . . . no one I knew . . . stretching a quick, impatient hand to her.

"Remus."

"Hush, hush," he said. "I will heal you with your own herbs. As you did me."

"But don't you see, my dear? I already am. The leaves of the monkey puzzle—they got in my eyes. Now I can see the moon. But you—who will look after you, little bird?"

"I will!"

Only the wind heard me. What did he care for a Faun with stubby hands? Wanderer, he would tell the woods. Gossiping, he would skim the thousand steps into the Valley of the Blue Monkeys; leap the palisade of the Fauns; rustle the hive of the honey bee: *Woods, your green is gone.*

Only the wind heard me. Never mind, she hated broken promises.

She had loved two kings; no, three. Daughter to Aeneas, beloved to Ascanius, mother to Remus. Halcyon, Phoenix, Woodpecker. She was always Green-O-the-Woods. At the last, I think, she was first of all the forest mother. Broken, she lay on her couch, her catafalque. Strangely I did not see her like a tree bereft at noon.

I thought of birds.

"I never meant to outlive her," he said.

"It isn't given a man to choose his years." Empty words for the emptying of love. "If it were, why, she might have chosen the brevity of a bee or a Faun and missed the best."

"This?"

"Before this. And after."

"Nothing."

"A wonder."

"What, Sylvan?"

"The Bird of Fire."

I heard his tears; I heard the bees beyond the open window gathering into a lamentation, the forest lamenting its stolen queen, its too late king. My people, the Fauns, believe that the bees speak only what is in our hearts, not theirs—our sorrows, our exaltations, not theirs. That their sound is always the same, workers about their predestined work, and it is we who darken or lighten it to our mood.

But then, you see, I was no longer a Faun. I was Remus' friend.

II

Romulus rested from being a king. He had ploughed the fortunate circuit of his walls and left a brief threshold of grassy earth: plain walls—stones interlocked and faced with mortar from lime, water, and sand; plain as a shepherd's hut, but tall and strong like shepherds who had been to war. Stripped in the torrid sun, he leaned on the plough, his hard thighs diamonded with sweat, his beard a glistening *v*. I looked for guilt and saw dominion.

With mattocks and shovels instead of staffs, his

men prepared to build: wall before house, house before temple, court, market. . . . Except for the piles of stone and the vats of mortar, they might have been warriors anticipating another war. They wielded the tools as one might wield a sword, aggressively, eager to thrust and parry, match iron with iron, instead of invite the earth and lift the stone. Romulus had captured the *numen* or magic of the gods. Now they must raise high walls and imprison the magic against the hazards of time, the envy of men without cities, the bodiless lust of the dead.

They sang as they dug. The truth of Rhea, the twins, the mothering wolf, had begun to blur into legend and shape itself exclusively into the lineaments of Mars. Heroism, it seemed, meant to hurl a spear and capture a throne, not to make laws and serve the gods. Swords, not staffs. Wolves, not birds. Romulus, not Remus.

> Romulus, sired by the spear god Mars,
> Nursed by the long gray wolf,
> Swaddled in valor, cradled in pride,
> Teethed on victory's sword. . . .

Celer led the singers, inharmoniously but lustily; he and his nameless friends. The song suited him; perhaps he had helped to write the rhymeless, graceless lines.

"Romulus!"

Romulus raised his chin from the plough, recognized his twin, and smiled.

"Yes, brother?"

"Romulus, your walls are useless. Your luck is gone. A murderer stands inside."

I hardly knew him for my friend. It was the first time that he seemed to have had no mother, not Rhea, the Novice, nor Mellonia, the Lady of the Bees, nor Larentia, nor even Luperca. Mars had sired him. Mars possessed him. In the temple of his undivided heart, division warred with love; the image of deity threatened to crack.

I had been drunk with Mars. I knew the look.

"Remus!" I reached to touch his arm, to gentle him from his rage.

I was afraid for him.

He might have been a Lemur, so utterly did he slip between my hands (Faun's hands, stubby and awkward. Had I reached less clumsily, perhaps . . . Ah, the road to the Nether Land resounds with Perhaps).

Then he jumped the ring and broke the magic.

I could only watch him with disbelief. I expected a thunderbolt.

"Celer!" The cry was a curse. "Celer, the stunted man! I have come to kill you."

And then they fought.

Lovers could not more intimately touch and lock, but death was the lover in that fight.

Like figures in the Nether Land, like Lemures, not flesh but flesh remembered in a dream, they beat the grassless dirt between the unbuilt walls; like mists embodied briefly into men, they whirled and strove; eternalized in a dream, in doom. Shadows in shadow land. All color seemed to drain from them: green from Remus' tunic, flax from his hair; brown from Celer, his sunburnt skin, his donkey face. All grays they seemed; grayly awhirl in that eternal war between blind chaos and unyielding order (except that each had borrowed the other's mask).

I wanted to join Remus in his doom. I wanted to shut the flat, unlovely eyes; restore the boy into the house of light; return the deity to his pedestal; crack the doom instead of the image.

I could not follow him across the ring. (Had he cried "Silver Bells," I still could not have jumped the fortunate ring.) I believed in gods. I entered through the gate; lost time, permitted doom. Perhaps impiety would have better served my friend.

Remus was strong if slight; young; his father fought with him. Motion, then cessation. . . . Figures ceased to whirl; gray drank color; standing green confronted fallen brown, separate but inseparable.

"Get up," said the boy. "I am going to kill you."

"Impious," shouted Romulus. "It is you who have broken our luck. Fight me, not Celer."

He snatched a shovel from his closest man—weapon disguised as tool—and raised its iron command above his head.

"Keep away from me, Brother. My quarrel is not with you."

"You made it mine when you broke my luck. Fight me, I say!"

Remus turned to Romulus but not to fight. To speak. I saw him start to speak his brother's name. I saw the flight of Mars; the temple indivisible, the gentle god restored to deity.

He turned into the moving shovel. Romulus, I think, had meant to strike his arm, his threat to Celer. He caught the metal in his face. The blow was meant to stop; at most to stun.

He caught it in his face.

The perfect features did not dim; the wide green eyes stared Dryad trees and Silver Bells and, at the last, surprise, as if to say,

"But I am Remus. . . ."

The hair, that miracle of sun, did not forget its fire; still, something was gone,

The luck from a city,

The light from a lantern shaped like a moon,

The woodpecker from its nest in the hollow tree.

He did not say goodbye (Remus, I can forgive your not outliving me, but no goodbye? It was not like you, friend. Memory feeds on morning's manna but at the last must starve for one good-night).

The cry belonged to Romulus. Stricken by worse than blows, he joined the dust beside his twin; side by side, the dark and the fair (but dark was life).

Once, in the forest, a she-wolf saw a shepherd kill

189

her cubs (I watched her see). All pain, all yearning, was the single cry wrenched from the vital organs of her frame, as if their swift, red pulsing could recall her cubs from death.

In Remus' hair, the stains were from the earth, the umber soil commingled with the flax. There was no blood, no wound. Only the luckless city, the lightless lamp, the nest untenanted.

I seized the hateful tool, the claw which borrowed strength to rend.

"Stand up! I am going to kill you."

He turned his face to me, wearily, as if it cost him pain; he, the king.

"Sylvan, I wish you would."

Perhaps I would have killed him. Except for a trick of light, a shadow slanting down the handsome face—well, some tricks are truths. I seemed to see the mother instead of Mars.

Faustulus laid his hand on Romulus' head. I had not seen him come to watch with us; he seemed to walk in quietude. (He said, a year ago, remembering Larentia, "Love is silences as well as speech. A little hut; a hearth against the cold: Speech is a formal guest, silence is at home.")

"My son, there is nothing here of guilt. You loved him best. He knew, he knew. Let me prepare him for the fire."

"Good. Hector but not Achilles. First I must make my peace with him."

"I will stay with Remus."

Shadows sat with us; then dusk, a sad companion; then the night, that grave sweet lady in the sable robe. The men dispersed in longing to their huts. Romulus was their king. Remus had been their son. Lights made fireflies of the open doors. No one laughed or sang; still, they had their hearths, their gathered warmth against the darkness which, in love with light, had stolen light's own prince.

Except Celer. I saw him leave the hill, he and his friends (no one, I think, had ever heard their names.) The forest though was not his friend.

A milk cow lowed with quiet urgency.

Ah, the old black cow we stole to start a war. She has no milk to give. But Remus guessed her pride; for him, the shrivelled udders seemed to spurt white gold. Is this the measure of a man—how many wait for him? Then Remus must be measured twice a god.

"He must have a roof," I said. "He never liked the dark. He said your mother's ghost had not been laid to rest."

"That was before we killed Amulius. I hope he learned to trust the dark. I cannot say. Mellonia's tree, perhaps? Someone must tell her."

"The tree is dead. Celer killed her. He and his friends."

Wolf-anger leaped behind his face. Protector, though, not predator. Good. For wolves were strength to him, and he must build and rule a solitary throne.

"Then that was why he jumped the wall. I could

not understand why he would break my luck. Remus, who loved the gods. I could not understand. Sylvan, they will die."

"I know."

"Tomorrow is revenge. Not now. Your cave?"

"There is no where else for him."

He lifted Remus in his royal arms, shields, not swords, and climbed the hill. He did not seem to tire. I envied him the weight.

"At last," I said. The walk, it seemed, had taken half the night.

"So soon?"

"Soon? Not to a Faun."

"Well. Then we must stop."

"*Sylvan.*" Under Rumina's tree, the Telesphori stood like rounded graves.

"Lordon?"

A lantern like a moon bobbed in his hand. I saw his pink and pretty face. He wore the flush of youth but age peered through his eyes.

"Celer," he said (a rounded grave, an executioner).

"Good." I did not ask the means. I liked to think that they were cruel.

He raised a silver flute—the lamp said dagger till I saw him start to play.

"Sylvan, shall we go into your cave?" Perhaps he heard the hooded mourners; he did not see them. He never took his eyes from Remus' face. The Book of Tages says: "No man can die, finally, until you cease to watch his face; the spirit hesitates to issue through the lips and show itself in naked frailty." Romulus was no Etruscan learned in mysteries. Magic? The unexplained, not the inexplicable. A god might sire a son to be a king, but Jove did not descend in showers of gold. A Dryad was a girl with pointed ears. He pacified the gods before he built his walls, but not from love. He signed a covenant with them: "For you this spell, this sacredness. For me, defense."

But he had found, it seemed, a need for mystery. He watched his brother's face.

"Here is his pallet."

"Yes. It smells of clover. Not yet though. There is not enough light. . . ."

"I have lit three lamps."

"The hearthfire then. My hands are cold. . . . Luperca. Does she understand?"

"How not? She mothered him. You too, but you forgot."

"How old she looks! Old Mother, you stood guard when we were babes. Suckled us like your own cubs."

She crouched away from him. She did not like the scent of Remus on his brother's hand. Her son was dead. His killer was not her son.

"Those pictures on the wall—he drew them?"

"Who else? Fauns can't draw. Our fingers are too thick. You saw them before."

"I did, didn't I? I forget. Gods. Rumina. That one, though, is new. The boy."

"Vaticanus."

"I know. Like the malachite. A man is judged by his gods. I am Mars."

"More," I said.

"What did you say, Sylvan?"

"Romulus, please. Set him down. He will grow tired in your arms."

"Of course."

Rumina's tree became a tower of song. The words, like agile crickets, crept into the cave:

> "I go," said the wind
> To a yonderland
> Where the dragon feeds
> From a Dryad's hand
> And the Centaur blows
> On a silver horn
> To call the unicorn.

It was the lamentation of the forest, as old as Saturn; sung for him when he departed for the stars and silver, bronze, and brass, like falling skies, descended on a land accustomed to a king whose mossy beard had nested singing birds.

> "Wind," I cried,
> "Like a vagabond,
> You drift and play
> In the blue beyond
> And dream your tale

Of a Centaur's horn
Which calls the unicorn."

But the wind, he laughed
In a secret way
And climbed the clouds,
And who shall say
If he hears the call
Of a silver horn
And the hooves of a unicorn?

"I don't understand," said Romulus. "Did the wind really hear the horn?"

"I don't know. Perhaps if he was a great hero."

"Do you think only great heroes find Elysium?"

"I'm not sure if there's room for the little folk."

"And Remus—what did he think?"

"He didn't want an Elysium where there weren't any little folk. He said he would rather stay with the Lemures. But he didn't think Elysium was under the ground anyway. 'Believe me, Sylvan, it's in the sky. That's where the gods live. The last is going back to them.'"

"But if you had to guess for yourself——"

"How can I guess? I haven't reached the top of the monkey puzzle yet. But then, I haven't stopped climbing either."

"You're talking mysteries, Sylvan."

"Yes," I said. "Isn't it time?"

I was tired. I had tried to comfort him. I did not have to forgive.

"I will look after him now." I knelt and pressed my cheek into his shoulder's cradle, where I had sheltered as a child from Romulus. Almost I thought to find another nest.

"Woodpecker," I said. "You scolded Mellonia because you had to outlive her. But I am the one you punished. All of your life was loving—except for this. Where is your city, my friend?"

"In me," said Romulus.

"In *you?*" He had no right to break upon my grief with lies.

I had never seen him weep. Weep, not cry, I say. Kings weep. Little folk cry. Still, there is no difference between their tears.

"Do you really think I want only walls and armies?" he said. "At first I did. This morning I did, when I lied about the birds. 'A city is first of all a fortress.' I said that to Faustulus, who disagreed. To Celer, who added, 'A camp for armies.' But then I had Remus. It seemed I would always have him. He was the luck of the city. Mine too. Whatever I did, he would still love me. He had always forgiven me before."

"This time too."

"You see? He was all I needed of gentleness. Now he is gone—unless I resurrect him in our city. A second Troy, Sylvan. Men will call her Rome to honor me and fear her legions in the ancient great—

Carthage and Karnak, Sidon and Babylon. But her roads will carry laws as well as armies. Scrolls as well as spears. Sylvan, don't you see? Remus will live in us. In Rome. Come back with me, little Faun!"

"Will the city have room for Silver Bells?"

"Silver or gold, whichever you like."

"Gold is best, but silver climbs to gold."

EPILOGUE

Where is the Bird of Fire? In the tall green flame of the cypress, the lifted flame of the oak, I guess his burning. In the second Troy athwart the Palatine, where Fauns can walk with men, I hear the distant thunder of his wings, woodpecker-swift. Always shadow and sound but not the bird. Always he climbs beyond my capturing, and the wind possesses his cry.

Where is the Bird of Fire? Look up, he burns in the sky, with Saturn and the Golden Age.

I will go to find him.

ACKNOWLEDGMENTS

I wish to express a particular debt to Alan Lake Chidsey's *Romulus: Builder of Rome* and Carlo Maria Franzero's *The Life and Times of Tarquin the Etruscan*.

Resemblances between my Valley of the Blue Monkeys and James Hilton's Valley of the Blue Moon are obvious but altogether accidental: the color blue; the libraries which contain the world's great books; the longevity of the inhabitants. I only discovered them when I heard a record of Ronald Colman reading passages from *Lost Horizon*. I think that the explanation is not that I unconsciously imitated a book I had read more than twenty years ago, but that both Hilton and I imitated the same Utopian myth.

ACE SCIENCE FICTION SPECIALS

Just $1.25 each

#1—From the Legend of Biel Staton
#2—Red Tide Tarzan & Chapman
#3—Endless Voyage Bradley
#4—The Invincible Lem
#5—Growing Up In Tier 3000 Gotschalk
#6—Challenge the Hellmaker Richmond
#7—Tournament of Thorns Swann
#8—Fifth Head of Cerberse Wolfe

Available wherever paperbacks are sold or use this coupon.

64A